Key West Shorts

Wesley Sizemore
&
Edgardo Alvarado-Vázquez

Key West Shorts
© 2018 by Wesley Sizemore and Edgardo Alvarado-Vázquez
cover photo by Edgardo Alvarado-Vázquez
Printed in the United States of America

ISBN 978-1-936818-47-1
Library of Congress Control Number: 2018950749

SeaStory Press
1508 Seminary St. #2
Key West. Florida 33040
www.seastorypress.com

Wesley would like to thank the members of the Key West Writers Guild for their support. The members of the Writers Scribes, past and present, for their understanding and editing suggestions. Elizabeth is looking down, editing pen in hand, smiling.

Edgardo would like to thank: his immediate family for allowing him to be himself and write. Wendi Ney, Allison Rich, Michael Nelson and Jill Hutchenson at the Key West Public Library; he bent their ears for editing, typos, misplaced commas and ubiquitous semicolons. The members of the Key West Writers Guild; as he tortures them with poetry, Spanish syntax and drives them crazy on purpose. The members of 'The Poetry Church,' Patty Tyfanny, Sheri Lohr, Malcolm Willison, Kalo (and Viking Lord, who's behind the curtain, most of the time); because they have to endure his diatribes about literature, films, and poetry.

They would both like to thank Lisa Mahoney for her friendship and insights.

Preface

I first met Wesley Sizemore and Edgardo Alvarado-Vázquez at the Key West Writers Guild. Soon, we became friends, both professionally and personally. We shared our work, ideas, and criticisms often over a bottle of wine and always with a smile.

They have put together this book of stories, Key West Shorts, and I am please to write this for them. They are both incredible writers with very different styles. Wesley writes like he's slashed his emotional soul and lets it bleed into the paper. Edgardo, on the other hand, weaves his characters into a skillful quilt filled with innuendo, wit and seduction that often leaves us fulfilled yet wanting for more. If you are looking to read something original about the quirkiness of the old Key West, this is the book you want to take home with you today.

Kenneth D. Michaels,
author of the award winning books:
The Gay Detective and *Only in Key West*.

Wesley Sizemore

You Choose
the Wine

In my Key West life, I was an electrician—what I'd done to put myself through college. It gave me more pleasure than teaching French, my profession 'up there' because, at the end of a job, I could look at the lights, the fans, the kitchen I had given life to and measure the worth of my labor. Besides, how could you possibly earn a living in Key West as a French major?

A contractor friend got me the electrical job at one of the Key West mansions in Old Town. It was a house built by one of the original salvors in the 1800s, the men who'd stripped the ships of their cargoes when a ship had had a fatal encounter with our reef. This house was one of the great beauties in town.

The wife, Natalie, was friendly. The husband, Owen, who had made, we'd heard, $400,000,000 in some kind of financial deal in New York, was distant and condescending, but condescending in ways that made me think "Social Insecurity."

One of my jobs was to wire the coolers for the husband's $300,000 wine collection with a back-up generator to keep the wine at 54 degrees if the power went out.

Christmas Day, a month or so after I'd finished their job, I was sick in bed with the flu, and
got a panicked phone call from the husband. The
wire drop from the street pole to their house had
caught fire and Keys Energy, the utility company, had cut the power to the house. Eight equally
privileged friends from New York were there for
dinner. Could I please, please help them?

I crawled out of bed, got in my work truck
and drove downtown. Their street was blocked
off by cops. The one waving cars away was Steve
Torrence, a gay cop I'd wired a house for. I rolled
down my window and stopped.

"Steve, I'm the one who has to fix this shit."
He waved me through.

I met the six utility company guys and told
them I knew what the problem was. I was surprised that they didn't look pissed off, but then
realized they were making triple time, paying for
every Christmas present under their trees.

When I pulled into the driveway, Owen
came out and asked me what I had to do. I heard
the generator laboring to keep his wine at 54 degrees (did that right) and told him to draw away
from me because I had the flu. He drew away but
followed me—at a distance—everywhere. The
problem was easy to find. One of the contractor's
laborers had sliced partly through an underground
conduit (buried too shallow) filled with the wires

feeding the guest cottage behind the main house. I'd warned the contractor and the laborer where the conduit was, so this pissed me off. The wires they'd sliced had finally fused, on Christmas Day, on Christmas Day, and the now-fried wires had caused an electrical surge (no disconnect breaker) back to and through the overhead wires and had set them on fire. Keys Energy had cut the service to the house when those wires, sucking unlimited current through themselves, started dropping fire onto the street.

I traced the blackened damage from the sliced conduit to the meter center (surprised it hadn't fried, too) and felt like a star as everyone watched me. Then I disconnected and capped the damaged wires in the meter can feeding the guest house, and told the utility boys to re-string the service drop to the house.

The wires re-connected—everyone standing away but me—the Keys Energy crew called in to Dispatch to re-energize the line. I turned on the main breaker and the lights above the dinner table came back on.

The utility boys left with their trucks. Owen came out and asked me how much he owed me, the look on his face showing that he expected the worst. Typical New Yorker.

"Owen, I have the flu and had to come over here on Christmas Day. Come on. There's not enough money in the world to pay for that. On the house. It's Key West. Merry Christmas. Have a nice dinner with your friends." He thanked me but gave me a look of incomprehension.

I did a few more service calls and general work for the couple, but the condescension I always sensed from Owen annoyed me. I am, my best friends tell me, arrogant, which I try to hide. I know my IQ—high—have lived in five countries and speak or read five languages and have three college degrees. I am an electrician in Key West because it's where I prefer to live, and construction work affords me a good living. Look down on me for it and I never forgive you.

Realizing their obligation to me for the Christmas service call, Owen and Natalie invited me to a dinner party at their house. I was told I could invite six friends.

A week before the dinner party, my nephew, Victor, visited. I had told him about Owen's wine room and Victor asked if he could see it. He was working in a wine shop part-time to pay for college and was curious to see a serious, private collection. I called Owen, got Natalie, and she said "Of course, come over."

Victor and I entered the wine 'cellar.' We walked past the multiple bottles of Lafite-Rothschild, Romanee-Conti, Petrus, several vintages of Margaux and Chateau d'Yquem. My nephew was impressed, both by the collection and also that I'd already tasted all those when I'd lived in Paris. Farther down the line, he stopped. "Damn! 1968 Vega Sicilia!"

"Serious, Victor? A Spanish wine! Spanish and California wine is what we used to get drunk on when I was in college because it was cheap."

"Uncle, someone brought French vines back to Spain determined to develop a wine as good as any of the French ones. They succeeded. If your host ever lets you choose the wine ask for this if you haven't tasted it. A bottle in my store goes for $2,000."

"Are you serious?"

"Serious. And what's the deal with that little table over there with the bottles on it?"

"That's the 'table of shame.' All the bottles of wine anyone brings to dinner that don't meet his standards get put there."

Victor laughed.

Owen knew I had lived in France and we had talked wine a couple times. When he asked me what wine I would like to be served at the dinner party, I told him I didn't expect one of the super-expensive French grands crus. "How about a Spanish thing? What about the '68 Vega Sicilia?"

He choked a bit, then nodded, not happily.

So, at an elegant dinner with five of my

friends, in a beautifully renovated ship's captain's house on Caroline Street, on a warm and fragrant February evening, eight bottles, $16,000 worth, of gloriously tasteful wine sat breathing on a side table. My friends and I agreed afterwards it was the best we'd ever tasted.

I was never invited back for work or dinner.

Edgardo Alvarado-Vázquez

David the Storyteller

After working in Silicon Valley for 28 years, I decided to cash in my 401K to write full time.

The first thing I did was read every single book that fell into my hands about writing. Celebrities as well as renowned authors have all written a "how to" from *Simple and Direct* to *Writing Down the Bones*. I read them all.

Everyone liked my stories. My friends have asked me several times to write them down. I started writing in long hand but it became cluttered soon. I couldn't organize my thoughts, then after wasting a couple of pads, I decided that the best way to work was on my laptop.

It was fitted with the latest writing programs. I brainstormed, typed the questions, ideas I wanted to explore. The characters started forming in my head. I cut with gusto, pasted with panache.

I needed to do research so I Googled my fingers for hours. I avoided outlines because I didn't feel comfortable fitting lots of information into such a rigid structure. I liked to be messy with my ideas. To clarify them, I added notes, drank wine. If a manuscript wasn't going well, I put it aside, then started another. Sometimes I wrote notes on the wrong manuscript. The pages started to flow. One afternoon I went to the park, tablet in hand. I needed to see the characters I wanted to write about. I took pictures of people doing all sorts of things, wrote notes about them. Then I went back to my desk and matched the pictures to the words in the computer. It was a clever process; I figured out that not all pictures are worth a thousand words. Some pictures elicit many thoughts, more words than most. Others brought forth nothing.

In one of those "how to write" books I found an emerald of wisdom: my characters must have magical qualities. That sounded right to me. Like an alchemist, off to the sunset, I went to create magic. My characters will fall in love on a whim, cure any disease real or imaginary, confer eternal youth; transmutate base materials into gold. They will use any cunning, mysterious, or creative processes to change the structure, the appearance of things. They will transmit messages in various forms, their gaze will come out of the paper to transfix the reader. I wrote a few pages, I waited for the combustible moment, for the ignition, for the blast, for the Big Bang. Nothing happened, not even a spark. I became a tyrant to my characters and since they did not want to give me magic, I cooked them slowly in what the Cubans called "caja china"; a contraption used to cook a whole pig.

A friend told me that the characters should have surrounded me. That maybe, if I changed my approach to that of an actor who had studied his next role, I might have gotten further. He said that every gesture, inflection was vital. I decided to start with him right then and there. I asked questions, wrote his answers, as well as the way he gestured when he spoke. I tried to develop my powers of observation to the fullest. We talked for four hours non-stop. The next time I invited him for another round of coffee, he made up an excuse. He has not talked to me since. After my third pal fled and alerted my other buddies, a support group was formed. They met every week and got restraining orders against me. I started grilling strangers in my favorite coffee house. The management banned me from entering.

I felt distressed; I went to a psychiatrist. My seventeen personalities were ganging up against me. They formed a caucus, wrote a manifesto against me, and presented it to my analyst in a hypnosis session. One of them committed Seppuku in that session to illustrate the point, three went into hiding and another one contacted the FBI on how to go into the FBI identity protection program. The shrink abandoned her practice, moved to a commune on Sugarloaf, started smoking from a pipe, and now paints pictures of Cuban cigars with the motto: "sometimes a cigar is just a cigar."

On an airplane going to a family funeral I interrogated my fellow passengers. After an hour, the one on my right faked sleep. The one on my left feigned a foreign accent and excused himself for his lack of English skills. An hour and a half loomed ahead, so I started a loose tale about my family. I went back a few years to my fifteenth birthday.

My uncle John had died in March, my great aunt in June and my cousin Myrna died that November in a car that went off a cliff in the countryside. These tales had been around in my head for a few years now. I felt discouraged. I couldn't seem to find a way to express what I wanted. I knew I didn't want it to be a recollection of family anecdotes. Again, using my tremendous computer and all the stuff in it, I tried to write out the connections between them. I drew genealogical charts. I tried to write where they were born, where they died. The captain's voice came on. Time to land. I named the file, saved it and closed the computer. Those few pages will be in storage for a while. I put the laptop under my seat, case closed.

While the plane was taxiing to the gate, I thought about writing short stories versus novels. I like short stories because I can control the plot;

the message is delivered by a punch. But to write a novel, you better have something to say. The words tricked me, eluded me. They did a Kokopelli dance in my head. I tried to prove to the words how smart I was before writing them. I wanted to gain perspective, a deeper irony and balance of emotions but I couldn't do it. The words became chaotic; they altered themselves provoked by the conflict. They became wicked, psychotic, totally evil entities without redemption.

My battle with the word was only paralleled by my battle with technology. The computer froze every couple of pages. I wrote the first paragraph two times from memory before I could save it as a document. My photo files were corrupted. A Trojan horse deleted first my cookies, then my html code. I took it as a sign; even my own computer hated me. But I wasn't going to give up. The war was on.

A couple of years went by, but still no book. I was looking for the rules for writing; there must be rules, they must be written somewhere.

In one of the writer's magazines, I read about writing conferences and seminars. That struck me as a great idea, so I talked with my accountant. We figured out I could do it without spending too much money. After considering a few options, I chose the Sandhills Writers Conference in Augusta, Georgia.

The people at the conferences seemed so far ahead of me. They had either learned to hide their emotions or they carried them, like torches, crosses with little wheels attached to the end of them. What the heck was I doing here? These places were magnets for writers but I didn't learn much talking to other struggling people. I didn't find the rules or the tools there. I was told that you don't talk books, you write them. But some of the seminars were okay. The meeting with publishers and the networking was good. I even got lucky a couple of times but that will appear in another story, not this one.

Still, there was no book.

One of the publishers in Augusta told me about a small literary seminar in Key West. Not that expensive, you arranged for your own accommodations. The groups were small and the participants had free rein over the sessions. You got the pieces in advance, selected by the writer/moderator then the group critiqued them. If the group was small, participants read more than one story. No structure, no questionnaires—I hate those. You came in Friday, met everybody, worked all day Saturday and the next morning. All work was finished around three, Sunday afternoon. That kind of seminar group sounded like my thing.

The first full day, a talented group of people presented pieces of sound quality. I read my short story about a female predator. The women in the seminar jumped at the chance to tear it apart. I took them to task. If I couldn't develop my sense of keen observation, I wouldn't let a group of pissy quasi-feminists destroy my story with their witty comments.

There was a woman from Chicago whose first book was accepted by a publisher; it was a memoir. A frustrated housewife that wrote about chores; THAT gave her the right, the authority to demolish my story? We discussed for a solid hour. I told her that she should go back to the Midwest and iron a few more shirts and write about it. Her jugular vein almost popped out of her neck. We argued until the writer/moderator reminded us that we had to move on. I wanted to jump across the table and bite his head off. I had tapped something, but I didn't know how to harness and use it. The discussion was so good I could taste the eager words in my mouth.

The second day was mediocre at best. A lot of incomplete pieces; I have no idea why the writer/moderator selected such pieces. I lost my patience with them.

For the second round, I presented my story of a house on Castro Street; it was a great story, it was complete. Of course in this middle-of-the-road group, no one understood.

There was a mature woman trying to write

a novel about Kentucky at the beginning of the century. What is there to write about horses and Kentucky? It was boring. I wanted to go after her, obliterate her; but I was polite to her only because of her age. The next one was a Puerto Rican guy with a story about his family. It was a vignette, for Christ's sake! Doesn't anybody know the difference between a short story and a vignette? What did a Puerto Rican amateur writer with bad grammar and using Spanglish know about writing? I tore him apart.

Then came my favorite broken piece of the session. A retired businessman from Oregon told us he had written an unpublished novel and adapted it as a short story for us. It was such a mess, no plot, no point of view, no character development and confusing dialogue. I had nothing to say. Again, the words left me. But the Oregonian, after a few irrelevant comments from the table, called on me to comment. I declined politely.

The table fell silent for a few seconds and then, they all pounced on me, hyenas smelling blood on the ground. Even the writer/mentor got a piece of the action. They all became literary critics paid to be ugly, though in this case, they had paid for their pound of flesh.

All of them lined up toward the center of

the force. I had the power of the room and if they wanted it, they had to wrestle it from me, pry it out of my clenched fist. This power was given to me; it's my right; so I swung my arguments like St. George against the Dragon. We argued about chances, coincidences, and the plot of my story. I stood accused of content without style, propaganda, premature writing and jerking off on paper. I particularly liked that one. The writer/moderator was my "coup de grace": I, the warrior, took his snakehead and cut it; destroyed his arguments in the sacrificial table. Blood rushed through my veins. It was decadent and I enjoyed the ride. I took all the poison in. I drank it with satisfaction.

I left the session exhilarated and decided to stay in Key West.

Still, there was no book.

Key West

Shorts

Wesley Sizemore

Was Key West Really That Crazy?

I am invited to an inordinate number of dinner parties through my work in construction. I meet newcomers to the island who all decide to make major or minor changes to their house, and we get to know one another—at least they think we do—and I get the invitation. I do it for business.

At each dinner party with new arrivals, I am thrown the same question, or a variant thereof: Was Key West in the old days as wild and crazy as they've heard?

I made the mistake my first time answering the question—everyone else from New England—of telling them about my first visit to Boca Chica bar on Stock Island and, when I was walking out at four in the morning, saw a whore on her knees blowing her customer. I had coughed to let the two know I was there, and the woman turned her head and yelled: "I'll get to you next."

I thanked the woman for the offer, I tell my listeners at the party, but told the woman that I needed to leave and her customer was leaning against my van. She scooted the man sideways so he was free of the van and, god bless her, didn't miss a stroke.

I had never been as embarrassed in my life as I was by the near total silence at the end of my tale, with everyone looking away from me. So now at parties with newcomers where someone always asks the inevitable question, 'Was Key West really that wild and different in the old days?' I have settled on three litmus-test tales about the disturbance at the Casa Marina (which is how the Key West Citizen, our hometown paper, referred to it), or the story of Henry and Alice, his pet goat, or the dancing rooster with the hard-boiled eggs. I choose which story to tell depending on how tight-assed the guests are and how much I've had to drink.

Deal with it or not, I have decided. Where the hell do they think they've moved to? A farther South version of Palm Beach?

I give them a little history first: The Casa Marina was commissioned by Henry Flagler, the man who built the railroad bridges from the mainland to Key West, and the hotel was built with the same German cement that Flagler built the bridges with. It is cement that shames what we use on the island today, in beams and buildings that don't last twenty years. The Casa Marina and the bridges have lasted a hundred years, and the community college built here with local concrete had to be torn down after twenty.

"Two Presidents—Harding and Truman—have given parties in the Casa Marina," I tell them, "and dozens of movie stars have stayed there, including Gregory Peck, Cary Grant and Rita Hayworth.

"When I moved here, the Casa Marina was closed except for a tiny bar on the Seminole Street side to keep the liquor license. Key West was that poor and devoid of tourists then.

"But five years after I moved here, the hotel was sold and the new owners decided to renovate and re-open it. If you haven't been inside, please visit. It is early 20th century elegance, a beauty. The coffered ceilings, alone, are jaw-droppingly beautiful.

"Anyway, to get back to my story...

"When it first re-opened, a friend of mine, Tony, was the reservation sales manager and desperate to fill the rooms and make the owners happy. Two months after the re-opening, he received a request from a group of doctors for a small convention. He gave them a group discount and booked a hundred men and women. What Tony didn't know was that they were a mix of doctors—obstetricians, urologists, surgeons and pediatricians—coming together to discuss, among other things, circumcision procedures."

At that, a few dinner guests start grinning, but most begin to look uncomfortable.

"Tony got a request for another convention meeting, from a group calling themselves USA. He booked them in, simultaneous to the doctors' convention, and got pats on the back from his boss: the hotel was full.

"Then, at three p.m. on Friday afternoon, as a prominent pediatrician was showing slides of babies tied down, comparing the efficacy of the three most common penis clamps used during circumcision, the doors to the hall slammed open and twenty men (and two women, Tony told me) burst in screaming 'SAVE THE SKINS, SAVE THE SKINS' and started throwing thousands of little circles of slimy, raw flesh at and into the audience. (We learned later that they had bought out the entire town's supply of raw squid rings.) When one fleshy circle landed on the pediatrician's lectern, then another hit her face, she ran off the stage.

"The protesters then grouped together and started down the main aisle chanting: 'DON'T CUT, DON'T CUT, SAVE THE SKINS' and threw T-shirts into the audience, T-shirts that had USA in big letters and, underneath, 'Uncut Society of America.'

"The police showed up and dragged them all off to jail.

"The Key West Citizen reported only that there had been a disturbance at the Casa Marina.

"The next night, my friend, Tony, came over and told me the whole story. 'John, seriously, USA? I'm supposed to know it's an anti-circumcision group, not a patriotic something or other?' He took a couple quick sips of the rum I poured him and was quiet for a minute. We looked at each other and then burst out laughing, stood up and started chanting USA, USA, USA, like we were cheering on our Olympic team.

"Tony lost his job, of course. I hired him on as an electrical helper, and the Casa Marina started to pursue legal charges against the squid ring tossers. But at every pre-hearing, the Key Westers in the court burst out laughing, so the Casa Marina dropped charges, the offenders were released, and the hotel was sold two years later to new owners."

When I finish my story, some people at the table are sick with laughter but most are not pleased.

If I have had enough wine at a dinner party where I have lost almost all fear of offending the other diners, I tell them the story of Henry Faulkner and his pet goat, Alice. You can go online and see a photo of the two of them.

"Henry was a very talented painter," I tell my audience, "showing in galleries in New York and Palm Beach. He lived in a small Conch house on Grunt Bone Alley, since re-named Peacon Lane when the rich started buying in. Henry was outrageously gay and usually went out dressed in women's clothes, accompanied by Alice. Bartenders, because Henry tipped well, always gave Alice a free bowl of bourbon, which she loved."

At this point in the story, some people are starting to smile, glad to be hearing a funny 'Key West in the Old Days' story.

"Tennessee Williams and Henry were friends, sharing available sailors and Conchs (the local inhabitants) and sometimes, each other.

"One afternoon, Tennessee (Tom, if you really knew him) walked over to Henry's for 'tea and conversation' (hard liquor and funny stories). Tennessee—Tom—knocked. Henry let him in and poured drinks. They swapped stories for a few minutes, then Tennessee jumped up and yelled: 'Henry, there's someone in your backyard trying to fuck Alice.'

"Henry jumped up, looked out and saw a shrimper in the standard white rubber boots, erection rampant, grabbing Alice's back legs, trying to mount her as she bleated in protest.

"Henry walked out and exploded in fury. 'Leave Alice alone, goddammit. Get in here and fuck me.'

"The shrimper, obviously drunk, turned and walked inside. Tennessee told the man to follow Henry into the bedroom and, laughing, pointed the way."

At the end of my story, I am usually embarrassed again, but tell everyone at the table to look up Henry Faulkner online and see the photo of him with Alice.

If I am truly drunk I tell my listeners the third story. A gay man gave a party at his house on Fleming Street for all his gay friends. An hour into the party, a naked man walked into the room where everyone was drinking, squatted down and began flapping his folded arms up and down and squawking like a hen. All conversation stopped and, when the hen saw he'd gotten everyone's attention, he squawked louder, turned and popped a hard-boiled egg out of his butt. He moved around again, flapping arms and squawking more, stopped again and popped out another egg.

By now, half the guests want to throw up and the other half was laughing uncontrollably.

Chicken made one more noisy trip around the room, popped a third egg out his butt and went back to the bedroom he'd come out of.

No one ever forgot that party, and, YES, Key West was that wild and crazy back then.

How could you not miss those days?

Key
West

Shorts

Edgardo Alvarado-Vázquez

No Working Title Yet (David the Storyteller Part 2)

I was working on a manuscript that I felt comfortable with. I had never thought of writing a memoir; I really wanted to write the great twenty-first century American novel. Something like *Gone with the Wind*. However, after trying for so long I still couldn't. So here I am with the story of my childhood.

It began as a writing exercise following Rita Mae Brown's *Starting from Scratch*. Damn her, damn her cats and damn her exercises.

I dug out the few pages that I had written on that same airplane trip to my cousin's funeral. I kept thinking, "I don't want to do this now. Why in the world am I going to write about my family?" My inner voice kept fighting with my brain.

"Using your family as an inspiration? You are crazier than I thought," Inner Voice said sarcastically. "They are so dysfunctional; they are delicious."

"Paying attention to you is what is crazy, not my family," I replied. "Maybe if I take some serotonin, I'll get rid of you for a while."

"Really, you want to get rid of me? How about the other voices? I'll just be replaced. Don't you get that?"

"Yes, I do, but I'll be killing each one of you softly; like the song." I started humming it out loud. "All I have to do is run my fingers through your hair and hum. As you sleep I can go back to my writing career."

"What writing career?" It was laughing hysterically now. "Have you published something I'm not aware of? Have I slept that long? Haven't you had enough punishment from those writing groups and workshops that you attend?

I kept typing as the argument continued. I didn't direct my out-loud musings to the computer itself; but I guess it took it personally. It started acting up and shut itself down. "Jesus effing Christ." I said out loud as I faced the blank screen of my computer.

After an hour and a half of trying to give CPR to my CPU, I got it half-working. But I couldn't open my document, and I didn't have a backup. I felt crisis mode in my gut but continued anyway. I went to the on-line computer help website. I thought it was a victory for my computer abilities; I wish I hadn't done it. At the website I found an 800 phone number and was connected to a person. Amazing, unheard of in the age of computerized customer assistance. But something was amiss.

In a musical Hindi accent, the guy said:

"Hello. My name is James Smith. How can I assist you today?"

"You're kidding me," I said amused. "Now, what's your real name?"

"James Smith!" James replied a bit peeved.

I'm accustomed to all the jokes about the customer assistance desk. I'm also very aware of my own accent, English not being my first language. I speak with an accent, I read with an accent, and I write with an accent; but I have never been faced with a customer service assistant with an accent.

"With whom do I have the pleasure of speaking today?" the voice on the other side asked.

"David Smith," I answered a hint of snarkyness in my voice. The irony was lost to James. "Where are you located?" I'm feeling awkward now.

"New Delhi." He was irritated. Like I should've known where he was.

"I'm so sorry," I said, hoping he wouldn't take offense to that response.

"How can I help you?" James was authoritative now. "I'm sorry if I sound assertive, it is my first day on the job," he added, conciliatory.

"Not to worry." Not thinking about the global economy, I felt guilty of harboring any animosity against someone that I didn't know. I thought about all the implications, funny or otherwise. I took a deep breath and dove in.

"A few minutes ago, my computer shut down. But after several attempts, I got it working, I'm not sure how. Now I can't open the document I was working on. It is important, help me!" I pleaded.

"Make sure you attached the AC adapter and power cord properly or that you have installed a charged battery," he stopped for a minute waiting for my answer. I knew he was working from a script. Once while living in San Francisco, I worked as a telemarketer for an hour. It was a painful memory.

"Check!" I said.

"Press and hold the power button for a few seconds," he continued reading.

"Check!" I responded.

"Did the computer start?"

"Yes."

"But when you press any key on the keyboard or touch the computer pad, nothing happens?"

"Yes, I told you that already."

"Aha!" he said less annoyed now. "You are probably in Sleep Mode and have a software or resource conflict. When this happens, turning the power on returns you to the problem instead of restarting the system. To clear the condition, press Ctrl, Alt and Delete simultaneously, or press the reset button." He was so happy. He forged ahead. "Clearing the condition may get you running by disabling Sleep Mode, but it won't solve a resource conflict, such as random access memory, disk storage, cache memory, internal buses or network devices. Read the documentation that came with the conflicting device or software and the 'Resolving a hardware conflict' chapter in your computer manual…" He was unwavering.

"What documentation? I haven't installed any new software or hardware. What are you talking about?" I said a bit exasperated. "The computer is not accessing the hard disk or my flash stick." Did he pay attention to what I said? No. He went ahead with his pre-scripted monologue.

"Your computer normally loads Windows from the hard disk. If you have a hard disk problem, you will not be able to start the computer. Press F10 while you turn the power on."

"What are you talking about? I'm not completely computer illiterate. I don't have a hard disk problem." I was ready to reach out and strangle someone. The computer displayed the WARNING RESUME FAILURE message I told him.

"It's your battery. The backup battery is discharged. To charge the backup battery, plug in the computer and turn it on for about seven hours," he said convinced.

"There is nothing wrong with my battery, I told you that already," I said, again trying to mask my rage.

"Make sure there is no flash drive attached. If there is one, remove it and press any key to continue. If pressing any key does not work, press Ctrl, Alt and Delete, or press the reset button to restart the computer. If the problem persists, try restarting the computer with the Matsushita Companion software from the cloud, or another reliable system disk in the CD drive."

I became annoyed and mumbled a couple of things in Spanish that I shouldn't have. Maybe because I knew that the call was being taped for quality assurance, I felt guilty and stayed on the line with the voice from New Delhi and a document that wasn't working. His tone of voice became a bit more soothing as he said, "It's very difficult to provide a fail-safe set of steps you can follow every time you experience a problem with the computer. Your ability to solve problems will improve as you learn about how the computer and its software work together."

I felt I was in a beginning computer class or something. I tried again, "Look, all I am trying to do is open the document that I was working on for the last three months. Can you help me with that problem?"

He stopped for a second, I heard shuffling of papers on the other side and he started to read again. "If problem solving is taking a long time, take a break. If you have been fighting to solve a problem for a long time, you are probably frustrated by now. Stand up and take a deep breath. Often, you can find a new solution to a problem just by stepping away from it for a few moments. The more you work with your computer, the more likely you are to encounter one or more problems. Do not panic! You can resolve them relatively easily."

I went into Spanish mode, which is what happens when I get frustrated. I was talking so fast and he was trying to respond. I poured out all the frustrations that I had with the computer, the phone call to New Delhi and the Matsushita Company in a couple of minutes. At the end I told him, "I am stepping away from the phone and taking a hammer to my computer."

In the middle of all the chaos and the apologies from New Delhi, he blurted out, "You have a corrupted document." I didn't know whether to cry, scream, or throw the phone against the wall. I hung up, that was it. I had lost my manuscript.

I was sitting at my desk in the bedroom. Beside it sits a smaller table with books, some paper work, a glass holding pens, pencils, Xacto knives, and several boxes that held my research for some projects, including this one, and printing paper. I was at the point of tears thinking of re-starting one more time. I took the box with the research and went down the stairs to my porch. My intention was to throw the research from the porch in a final act of cleansing and purification. I didn't think about where the papers where going to land and the subsequent cleaning process, but those were minor details at the time of my anguish/anger mode.

As I walked toward the porch, the sun in a beautiful gleaming ball was blinding me. As it went down, I channeled Scarlet O'Hara in the last scene from *Gone with the Wind*, put the box back on the floor of the porch and said aloud, fist clenched in the air: "After all, tomorrow is another writing day."

Now there was no document, and still no book.

Wesley Sizemore

Saying Good-Bye to
Reinaldo Arenas

I was seventy-one now and saying my annual good-bye to Reinaldo for probably the last time. It was a full-moon night in December, the month of both his birth and death. I walked past the concrete imitation buoy that announced the Southernmost Point, where hundreds of tourists now lined up every day of the year to have their picture taken.

At this time of night, I was alone, I thought. Under a bad streetlight's flickering, I shuffled my way into the cold and shallow water past the tiny concrete 'phone booth' where, a century ago, the Havana-Key West undersea telegraph cable had come ashore. I was there to launch what I held in my hands when I stumbled on an underwater rock, yelped, and almost dropped my tiny cargo.

"Are you okay?" a man's voice called out. I hadn't seen his approach from behind me on Whitehead Street.

"Yes, thank you," I answered, annoyed at my ritual being interrupted.

"You're welcome, but can you tell me what you're doing. What's that in your hands?"

"Can you help me back out?" I asked as I

shuffled backwards towards the sidewalk, my foot in pain.

"Of course."

With him holding an elbow, I backed out of the water and walked over to the buoy and leaned against it. The flickering street light revealed a good-looking man, in his thirties I guessed.

"What's that you're holding. What are you doing? Looks like a toy boat. I'm John, by the way," and he extended his hand. I put down what I was holding and shook it.

"I'm Wayne."

John's voice was kind. Tell him what I was doing and why, or not? What did this 'look-down' generation know of gay and political persecution?

"Please tell me what you're doing," he asked again. "I'm curious. But if I'm annoying you, I'll leave. I only wanted to help. I thought you were in trouble."

"Okay, I'll tell you because I was in trouble and you did help me.

"Many years ago my partner, Thomas, and I were caretakers of that house," and I pointed to the pink house, Southernmost House, next to where we both stood. "One night, we were out in the front yard watering the plants and heard loud sobbing outside over by the Point, here, right here, where we're standing, right here. Back then, this phony, concrete buoy wasn't here, just a small, hand-painted sign, white-paint on weathered wood hanging on the Navy's fence over there with an arrow: HAVANA-90 MILES. Tourists kept stealing the sign so the city built this stupid buoy.

"Anyway, I walked out to the yard and came over and saw a man on his knees throwing something out of a suitcase into the water, crying in a way I don't like to hear. I asked him what he was doing.

"He didn't answer at first but, a minute later, still throwing something that looked like dirt into the water, let loose a stream of Spanish I couldn't follow, except for 'idiota, amor de mi vida.' Then he threw the suitcase against the chain-link fence that the HAVANA sign hung on and began sobbing louder.

"Nut case or human in need? I always err on the side of human in need and approached closer and asked him if he needed help and would he please come inside with me and have a drink.

"He left the suitcase, reluctantly, and got up and followed me into the house. Inside, I gave him a stiff rum-and-coke and explained to Thomas what I'd seen.

"Our Cuban guest stared into his glass, drank it down in three gulps, and I gave him another.

"I am Reinaldo," he said, when he'd emptied the second drink and I gave him a third. I translated for Thomas when he switched to Spanish. "I am a writer who escaped Cuba with my boyfriend during Mariel, and I begged him to move here with me from New York because this island is so close and so similar, but he never came. Then he killed himself."

"Thomas went over to his sofa and put an arm around him."

"So I came here to throw my friend's ashes into the sea so they would wash across to Cuba, our home," and he started crying. I was crying when I translated it.

"Then he jumped up. 'Muchisimas gracias,' but I need to walk and be alone.'"

"He left the house, and Thomas and I both worried."

"Three years later, a friend of mine gave me *My Deep Dark Pain Is Love,* a collection of gay Latin-American short stories. Some were bad, some were okay and some were brilliant. Gay doesn't automatically give you talent, I think. But when I started reading one, *The End of a Story,* about a gay man, Reinaldo Arenas, spreading his lover's ashes off Southernmost Point in Key West, here, right here, talking to the ashes, I realized it was the sobbing man I'd invited into Southernmost House for a drink and comfort."

"Are you serious? Reinaldo Arenas!"

"Yes, Reinaldo Arenas."

"A while later, his book, then the movie, *Before Night Falls*, came out, and when I saw the price that man, the man we'd invited in for a drink, had suffered for his writing and for expressing his natural sexuality, I had a new hero.

"Reinaldo and I had parallel lives, John, both suffering the hell of being gay and dissidents; he against Castro's ego-maniacal tyranny and I forced into exile for refusing to serve in Vietnam and getting beaten up once by a man who pretended to want me but wanted my wallet. But Reinaldo paid an infinitely greater price, then got AIDS and committed suicide. Thomas, my partner, who loved the book and movie as much as I did, also died of AIDS.

"So, every December, on the anniversary of Reinaldo's birth and death, I come here to Southernmost Point and launch a cardboard boat towards Cuba—that's what I have in my hands—and the sail is a piece of paper I've written one of his poems on. And I recite some of his translated poetry as I walk out into the water. The man and his suffering cannot be forgotten.

"So, John, if you don't mind, help me launch this boat toward an island that should have embraced his brilliance. This is what I do every year."

John removed his shoes and we stepped back in the water, negotiating around the stones, and I began reciting from memory:

'I am that repulsive child that improvises
a bed out of an old cardboard box and
Waits, certain that you will accompany me.'

We reached a place where we could both easily stand. I set my little boat with its ballast of sand on the water and recited the lines on its paper sail:

'As long as the sky whirls
You will be the truth of myself,
the song and the venom,
the danger and the ecstasies,
the vigil and the sleep . . .'

John helped me back out of the water again.

"Wayne, I've just moved here but, please, can I join you for this every year? It's so beautiful that you do this, honor that man this way."

"Yes," I answered, "I could use a friend. All mine are dead now."

He put an arm around my shoulder. We turned to look back at the water. A breeze had caught the moonlit sail and moved the boat out to the sea that was Reinaldo's 'My Jungle and My Hope.'

John and I watched for a couple minutes, then began walking down Whitehead Street, talking softly, knitting together the beginnings of a friendship.

Edgardo Alvarado-Vázquez

The House on
Fleming Street

To Ms. Florence Yaple because I love you;
To Ms. Florence Maloney because I've never met you,
but we would've been good friends

I had decided not to evacuate during Hurricane Irma. Why? I really didn't have a choice. I didn't have the money to go to a hotel with my two little mutts; two wire-haired terriers. They're white and fluffy and full of energy. I got them at the local SPCA.

I prepared the inside of my apartment, the best way I could and talked to friends who were staying. Conchs don't evacuate because the government makes it so difficult to come back that most of them stay. The apartment management company was boarding the windows and doors.

Ms. Florence is tall with the textured skin of an avid gardener. She wears the same kind of clothing, almost a uniform: flowy tunics in bright primary colors and black Capri pants. She has been living at her house on Fleming St. since she came back from the war in the 1940s. We met at work, at the Key West Library where she volunteers re-shelving books and getting discarded ones for the sailors at the Boca Chica station. She also volunteers at other venues in town. How she does it is unknown to me; but she goes around her chores with the precision of a scientist.

"I heard you're staying," she said as she approached me at the circulation counter.

"Yes, I don't have any money to pay for a hotel, and I have my babies. There aren't many places that take pets without high fees."

"Why don't you stay with me? As long as the dogs stay in your room and you clean up after them, there's no reason to spend it alone. I have plenty of room."

"But I don't want to impose."

"Child, why would I have asked, if I thought you were imposing. It's decided. And you won't be the only one staying there. Some other friends will join us."

The company that manages the apartment building came early and boarded the windows. I took the plants from the porch and put them in the kitchen sink and gave them a good soak. Who knew when the water would come back on? I wasn't going to show up empty handed—it's not polite. I packed everything that was easy to prepare from the fridge, threw out the rest; without electricity, it was going to spoil anyway. I crammed a small bag with food for the dogs, t-shirts, shorts, some bras and undies. I guess that the possibility of losing my housing was far from my mind.

We arrived Friday night around seven; I got the far right bedroom on the second floor. The dogs won't bother much in that corner. Ms. Florence had dinner ready. We put away the food that I brought in and ate. I also brought two bottles of wine. Ms. Florence doesn't drink but she is okay around people who do. She loves to talk and tell stories. I got most of her biography that night.

"During the war, I was in the Nurse's Corps and got a commendation from the government; and I met Frank, he was in the Navy," she pointed at his picture. "We bought the house on Fleming Street after the war. The fact that it was a hospital during the first decade of last century was a happy coincidence. Frank died twenty years ago. I don't like to talk about death. It's been around me way too long."

I was looking at my reflection in the glass of wine, "Were the renovations difficult? Turning a hospital back into a home is quite a task."

"We were young and the world was our oyster. You couldn't say no to Frank." Ms. Florence looked at his picture again. He became friends with the Thompsons, owners of the hardware store, on Grinnell and Caroline streets. They even helped us a couple of times. The house ended up with four bedrooms, three upstairs and one down here around the living room and three bathrooms. I've been sleeping downstairs since the eighties;

I don't do stairs anymore. But the bedrooms upstairs are clean. The rest of the guests will arrive tomorrow. We'll be fine. I'm worried about the garden. Wilma decimated it; I wonder what Irma will do." She looked at the backdoor. It was the only one that wasn't barricaded. I thought about the fact that the rooms are clean and that she hasn't been upstairs since the eighties. But I rendered this little useless digression to the fact that I was feeling sick and stashed it away in my mind. For sure she had a cleaning service.

"Ms. Florence I don't feel that good tonight. I'm going to bed."

Ms. Florence felt my forehead, "Seems like you have a touch of fever. Rest will take care of it. I'll turn in too."

It was a restless night. I had a low grade fever and a couple of nightmares. Binky, my little girl, sensed my mood and got really close to me. Mork took charge of the bottom right corner of the bed.

Saturday morning Ms. Florence and I did a final walk around the property making sure that everything was ready. Around noon, the rest of the boarders arrived: Peggy, her wife Myrna Blue and their dog Lady, another rescued dog, a Whippet with a very dignified look. They took the room on the opposite corner to mine; thankfully Lady is a much better-behaved dog than mine are. Martha Stewart—yes that's her real name—Ms. Florence's best friend. Now she lives in New Town. Since her last stroke, she's had a live-in caretaker named María and her daughter, little Mary. Cotton, Mary's bunny, came in her carrier. They took the middle bedroom upstairs.

Once you put six women, a child, three dogs and a bunny together, all sorts of mayhem ensues. The kitchen has a gas stove, very convenient when there is no electricity. In the middle sits a beautiful mahogany table; it became ground zero. I still had my fever and I thought a glass of wine might help. Peggy and Myrna drink so I was in good company; they had brought their bar with them. Martha doesn't drink either, but tonight she made an exception and accepted a glass of wine. Peggy, a retired chef, demonstrated her culinary prowess and created a fantastic dinner. We became a family bonded by a natural disaster but thick as Elmer's glue.

The wind was picking up speed outside while inside the mojitos and the wine flowed. Ms. Florence's stories were at the center of a beautiful evening. She told us about the changes she has seen in the town; the fluctuations in its fortune, the corruption and the first Fantasy Fest. "I don't parade much," she added "the only parade I do now is on Veteran's Day. I carry Frank's picture."

My second glass of wine didn't help and, on top of my fever, a headache started to grab hold.

"Peggy, dinner was incredible, thanks; I'm not feeling well, I'm going to bed."

"Let me feel you," Ms. Florence said. "Yep, fever still there, just like yesterday."

I could hear them by the time I laid down. Binky snuggled on my pillow and licked the back of my head. I'm always awed by how perceptive pets are to the feelings of their owners. Mork parked himself in the same spot as last night. The electricity was out.

By midnight the windows started rattling. I could hear the rain pelting the metal roof of the house. Somehow, that noise didn't bother me too much; it reminded me of the storms I'd been through in Puerto Rico. My fever increased. I knew it was going to be a long night. I tossed and turned; Binky was keeping track of my movements and jumped in sync. Every bone in my body, and a couple of places I hadn't thought about in years, hurt. I looked toward one of the windows. The wind had partially opened the shutters. I could see a little of the outside. The rain was falling horizontally, coconuts and branches flew by, and in my stupor, I could swear I saw a fridge in the air. I'm not sure but it was a big white box. Every time a tree fell, the dogs would jump and bark. I'll never forget the sound of the wind.

The room filled with light. I staggered out of bed and, without thinking went to the wall to turn off the light. I forgot the electricity was out. I felt a hand on my shoulder.

"Child you're burning up. You better go back to bed."

Binky and Mork stopped barking; they just went to the same positions. My head hurt. I couldn't make out who it was, but I supposed it was Ms. Florence. She guided me back to bed, pulled up a chair and sat down beside me. I went back to a lethargic dream; I couldn't sleep, but I heard her coming and going around the room. Her long skirt was noisy too; do women still starch their skirts? I was going in and out of consciousness, was I dreaming all this? My head was on fire. I felt a cool compress on my forehead. The noise outside increased, decreased, the light came in and out. The dogs remained quiet. At some point, I heard a lullaby in Spanish, from my childhood. Maybe I was dreaming. Another tree fell outside. Daybreak, my fever broke. I slept till eleven.

When I made it downstairs; Binky and Mork went after Lady barking and running circles around her. Lady growled at Mork and put one of her paws on top of Binky. End of game.

Myrna Blue put a cup of coffee in my hand. "You look like shit; what happened to you last night?"

"Thanks," I replied, "You look like a dandelion too. I had the worst night of my life. Where's

Ms. Florence? I have to thank her for her help."

Myrna gave me a puzzled look and said, "As soon as she could, she opened the back door and stepped out to check the garden."

"You want to thank me for what?" Ms. Florence came in cleaning her hands with a towel. "The garden is a mess. It will take months to recover. Don't venture out, looks like every single tree in the street fell down. You guys can stay here for a few days if necessary."

I put my cup down and gave her a hug.

"Child, get off me! Don't you see I'm dirty and sweaty? What has gotten into you?" she protested.

"You were so kind last night," I held her hand. "And I didn't know that you knew Spanish, which was the sweetest part; my mother used to sing the same lullaby to my younger brother."

"I don't have the faintest idea of what you're talking about. Have you lost your senses? And you need to eat something; you look like Elena Hoyos when they found her in Von Cosel's house."

"My fever spiked, it was a horrible night with the storm; everything ached. I guess that I was tossing and turning so much that you came upstairs to check on me." I picked up my cup and sipped. "You stayed for a long time."

"You saw her!" Ms. Florence exclaimed. "Since I don't go upstairs anymore, I haven't seen her, I don't think she likes the downstairs."

"Peggy," Myrna Blue called as the bacon sizzled in the frying pan, "Peggy, Martha, María get your butts over here. You've got to hear this."

The mahogany table filled up. Myrna Blue kept working as Ms. Florence filled us in on the details. There were eggs, bacon, biscuits with gravy, grits with cheese and coffee.

"In the 1860s Dr. John Maloney opened the first drugstore in Key West. He married his high school sweetheart Louise; I don't remember her last name. And then came the Maine explosion and the war with Spain. The Maloney family owned a few properties in this block. When the Navy started bringing back the wounded and the dead from Cuba, Maloney turned this property into the hospital."

"How come you know all these details?" Peggy asked.

"Frank was a history buff, he dug out all the history. The Maloneys are still in town but their last name has changed." Ms. Florence answered with a smirk. "But I have other sources."

"Around 1905, Mercedes Rodríguez arrived in Key West from La Habana. She was going to marry a wealthy tobacco grower from one of the oldest families in Cuba, but he left her for another more suitable match. Mercedes arrived broken-hearted and found a position at the drugstore. Mercedes was trained in La Habana as a nurse in the convent of the Ursulines. It wasn't difficult for her to get selected as the head nurse when Louise died of consumption. In 1908 the hospital was renamed Louise Maloney Hospital in her honor."

"There were no other hospitals in Key West at the time?" I was stuffing a piece of biscuit in my mouth.

"I'm not sure. There might have been one on Southard Street but this was the first private one. John kept it going during the twenties but when he died, the family didn't want to continue and the hospital was sold in 1925. That same year, without any prospects for her life, Mercedes hanged herself in the far right corner bedroom."

"No wonder," I said, peeved, "she was with me the whole time."

"The story doesn't end there." Ms. Florence's eyes were shining. "My Frank always said that the story was hogwash, but I know for a fact that he saw her too. He just wouldn't admit it. We didn't have kids. After Frank died, Martha, my friends at the church and the owners of the store beside the house looked after me. My biggest problem was at night. I didn't want to be alone. So I moved my bedroom to the right corner and Mercedes started spending time with me. She was lonely too. I always knew when she was coming because of the noise her dress made when she walked."

"I heard the same noise when she was moving around the room." I was sipping my coffee.

"After she arrived from Cuba, she never laid eyes on any other gentleman other than her patients. She never had a need for clothing; her uniforms were all she had. She washed and starched them by hand. After the hospital was sold in the twenties, the new owner changed it back into a house; and Mercedes stayed taking care of it. That owner died in 1946 and we bought and restored it."

Everybody went back to their houses and their lives. Martha Stewart had one of the only working telephones in town. She made it available to anyone who needed it. When the bill came it was high. The mayor of Key West found out and paid the bill out of his own pocket. I stayed at Ms. Florence's house a couple of extra days until I received a phone call from the management company announcing the apartment was ready. I didn't feel uncomfortable in that room knowing that Mercedes would take care of me. I slept like a baby; Binky and Mork didn't bark either. The last afternoon as I picked up my bag I said, "thank you Mercedes, thank you for letting me sleep in your room. Please take care of Ms. Florence. Can you please go down to the first floor and talk to her?" I opened the door, Binky and Mork went out first and as I began to shut the door behind me, I could hear the ruffled noise of a starched skirt.

Michael Cucumber

There is a line that raced through the town in the late '70s, through the gay community first, then got picked up by the tribes of construction workers.

When gay people, mostly from big cities, started moving to Key West in serious numbers back then, what they didn't realize at first was that one of the realities of life in a small town was that there were no secrets, apart from the hidden corruption of the people who ran it.

Cheating lovers, gay and straight, after a quick fuck that may or may not have touched more than the body, would try to sneak a meal out together and usually chose the Hukilau on Roosevelt Boulevard. It had dim lighting, a 'faux' Polynesian décor with some thatch here and there, tropical blue and pink paint, a 'pu pu' appetizer platter, and lots of coconut-fried seafood.

It was there where I first learned the smallness of the town when I tried to sneak a dinner with my friend, a young male beauty, because we were approaching the 'Are we going to get together, or not?' moment for him. He was beautiful and great sex, and, yes, I was cheating on my lover of three years.

Looking deep into Doug's eyes, I started to tell him that I cared for him and that we'd always be friends, the prologue to a gay man kicking a 'trick' away, when I was interrupted by the hostess seating two men at the table next to us. When I looked over, I was shocked: it was Thomas, my lover, with a man I didn't know. Thomas and I glared at each other for a minute.

I spoke first. "Well, do we do this the American way and stand up and start fighting? Or do we do it the French way and you join us at our table and we all have dinner together?" Thomas laughed first, and we did have dinner together and then a four-way afterwards, and our illicit lovers became lovers and Thomas and I rode it out and stayed together.

A star arrived on the island shortly after my dinner at the Hukilau: Michael, whose last name always seemed vague or changed and who often ate there with varying partners. What didn't change as it went through the gay grapevine was the news that his member was as big as the biggest cucumber you'd ever seen, and it got rock hard. He was also model beautiful.

People started calling him 'cucumber dick.' He would go to the Monster disco on Front Street and walk into the men's room and hang it out. He charged ten dollars to look at it and slapped away anyone who tried anything more. He made enough money to pay his rent.

Arriving on the island at around the same time was an elderly, gay multi-millionaire from New England, but of French-Canadian descent, Ferdinand Coudert, who insisted on the French pronunciation of his last name (Koo-Dare). Ferdinand—Ferdy—to his fellow multi-millionaires. He was a gay 'bottom,' and when word reached him of a cucumber-dick 'top' in town, he sent troops out to find him. They found him, Michael.

Ferdy bought a Conch mansion on Caroline Street and hired Michael to supervise work on the house, and they became a couple. I was called over to do the electrical work and Michael, acting now like crowned royalty, led me through the job.

Two gay realtors, partners, Clay McDaniel and Fred Cole, had sold Ferdy the house. They plied him after the sale with dinners and contacts to bind him to them, and got invited to spend part of the summer with the two of them in Monaco, in the ten-million-dollar apartment Ferdy owned there.

Fred and Clay immediately sensed tension on their first arrival in the Principality, especially in restaurants where dinner for four was always over $3,000. Michael was unhappy.

On the third day of their visit, during a catered dinner at home, Ferdy gave in and begged: "Michael, I can't stand seeing you like this. Please tell me what's wrong."

Michael sighed, dramatically. "Ferdy, everyone in Monaco has a Rolls, and we're riding around in a Mercedes. Do you have any idea how cheap that makes me feel?"

"Oh God, Michael, I was so worried that it was something else. Is it really only because of the car?"

Michael nodded.

Fred and Clay watched as Ferdy went to the phone and had the concierge call the Rolls-Royce dealer.

"Wait," Michael yelled across the room. "I don't want one of those ugly, new, snub-nosed things. I want a Silver Cloud, the ones with the long hood."

It took Ferdy two hours of calls out and back, and $200,000 and a car swap, but a classic, gray, Silver Cloud, complete with chauffeur, awaited the four of them as they left the building the next evening for drinks and dinner at the Casino. The chauffeur opened the doors. Ferdy and Michael sat in back, and Fred and Clay sat in the jump seats facing them.

"Happy, honey?" Ferdy asked Michael, patting him on the leg.

"Yes, Daddy. Love you," and gave the old man a quick peck on the cheek.

Back in Key West, Fred and Clay told the story to a few of their friends, swearing them to secrecy.

Of course, they told everyone.

It exploded across the island, first in the gay community, then among gay men doing construction work, and then everywhere. For weeks, on job sites when a construction worker would be cursing a job going wrong, a fellow worker listening to the cursing would ask: "What's wrong, honey? Are you unhappy? Why?"

The man questioned would fake a limp wrist and answer "Because everyone else rides around in a Rolls and I get hauled around in a Mercedes. Do you know how cheap that makes me feel?" and the entire job site would explode into laughter.

Ferdy sold the house in Key West and he and Michael moved permanently to Monaco when they heard the story had been circulated, but also because Key West was too 'low rent' for Michael now.

But even today, every once in a while, when old-time residents are eating and drinking together, and one of them starts to rant, his or her friends at the table laugh when it has gone on long enough, and one of them says: "Do you know how cheap this Mercedes makes me feel when everyone else has a Rolls?"

The line still causes an explosion of laughter on the island.

Edgardo Alvarado-Vázquez

An Awkward
Key West
Story

To Dana Salinero with love and friendship
To Roxanne and Michel with gratitude

Tonight we're celebrating my birthday and Dana just called.

"Cha Cha, don't forget it's at my house tonight. We are going to rumble!"

"Yes, yes, I won't," phone vibrates; it's Anne; it went to voicemail.

"Girlfriend, we're going to tear it down. Don't be late."

Kathy sent a text, "I guess I'm not getting out of it, so might as well show up."

I texted back, "And you might even have fun!" I'm careful with Kathy; she lost Jack a few months ago.

Dana, Kathy, Anne and I have been friends since high school. We went to FSU together, graduated, and came back to Key West.

Kathy is all about the arts community; she's a sculptor and a painter. She has had a couple of shows in town alone and with other artists. She is involved in the theater and she writes. Dana is a massage therapist and owns her own spa. Anne teaches English and reading at the local college. I run a financial consulting firm from my house. We have all done okay for ourselves and still enjoy each other's company. We have been through several boyfriends and girlfriends: a total of six marriages and one widowhood.

I go through the rest of my day dreading the impending celebration, but I want to see the girls. Even though we live in the same town, we don't see each other as much as we could. Two clients later and one long, long conversation with one of my colleagues in Boston, it's four o'clock. I'm ready for my glass of wine. My home office is a little messy. Today I don't care. I take a long shower, put on some comfortable shorts, a t-shirt and a new pair of tennis shoes, the last a present from myself via amazon.com. I take a long time applying my make-up.

As luck would have it, tonight there's a big football game on TV. Dana's girlfriend and Anne's husband will be out of our space in the den. We will have the rest of the house for ourselves.

The drive to Dana's is relaxing; I'm late, of course. Boca Chica Road still has the charm that is characteristic of other parts of the Keys that aren't overbuilt. There are patches of wild green grass, mangroves, marshes and the abandoned Navy missile silos give it an eerie feeling. Dana and Silvia, a sheriff deputy, live at the end of the road. When giving directions to her house she says: "If you see the homeless or the nudist, you went too far." Still, it's a long way from US1.

The phone rings; the Bluetooth connection picks it up and sends it to the radio.

"Cha Cha where are you?" Dana chimes, "you're late."

"I know, I know, long conversation with Boston in the afternoon. It had to be done. Can't say no to money."

"Silvia made your favorite empanadas and you don't want to disappoint her. Next time she sees you speeding on US1 she might not look the other way."

"Is she wearing her uniform tonight? I might be in the mood," I changed my voice pitch.

"Dejate de comemierderias!" she protested in Spanish. She reverts to her mother tongue when she's uncomfortable; it's kind of cute.

"Where're you?" stronger voice now.

"In the middle of Boca Chica; this dammed road is so long. Relax; I'll be there in a few."

"Ok, hurry up," click.

After a few more twists and turns on the road, I get to the house. It's big by Key West standards. It was built by Dana's father in the seventies, and it shows some of the kitsch decorative options of the eighties. A semi-circled double staircase welcomes me. Every time I face that staircase, I think "how Cuban."

Many years ago, one of my aunts showed me a photo of her "quince," the Hispanic equivalent of your debutante's party. She was at the top of a similar staircase looking like a bride's cake in a white tulle gown. Going down each side of the staircase were fourteen of her girlfriends from the Ursulines private school in Havana dressed in their finest gowns; each one escorted by a tuxedoed young man from La Salle school.

My moment is interrupted by Dana's overly nasal voice.

"Cha Cha, you arrived. Two more minutes and I would have sent Silva down the road to rescue you," she added in a very low voice. "Damn girl, you look good," she adds.

"Nothing like a shower and 'Nair' for my short shorts look," I reply showing some leg skin.

"Let's get the partee started!"

"Stop pushing girlfriend, I'm coming, I'm coming. Am I keeping you away from your drink?" I protest.

"As a matter of fact, you are. Everybody else is here. Go ho."

Raúl, Anne's husband, and Silvia are enjoying the game upstairs in the den. The party is only starting downstairs.

"Here" said Kathy as she gives me a glass of Pinot Gris, my favorite wine. Anne gives me a hug and pours some of her Chardonnay down my arm.

The volume of the music goes up. We always start in the eighties and go down the years from there. Tonight it's Whitney Houston's *'Its Not Right'* followed by Alicia Cox's *'No One Is Supposed to be Here.'* The dancing is fun and furious and the wine goes down easy.

By the time we get down to Diana Ross's *'Love's Hangover'* and Tammy Wynette's *'Stand by Your Man,'* the game upstairs is in a commercial break and Silvia comes down and dances with us. We were at *'Stop in the Name of Love.'* Raúl stays in the staircase and watches. The sound keeps going up and up and unbeknownst to us, one of the neighbors is partaking of our party unwillingly. She contacts the non-emergency number of the Sheriff department.

Greg Johnston is on his cruiser going down US1. He had just clocked a motorcyclist doing eighty southbound on Sugarloaf. After a brief chase, the BMW stops and it turns out to be the art director at the local newspaper. He gives her a warning. When the call comes in over the radio, 'some kind of disturbance was going on Boca Chica Rd.,' Greg pauses for a moment.

"Do you want to finish the night with a disturbance?" he asks himself. "Sure, there are better things to investigate this late at night." He radios dispatch and says he'll take it. The address sounds familiar, but he is relatively new to the job and doesn't think about it much. When he is getting closer to the house, he can sure hear the music. Silvia's squad car is parked behind the house, so her guests could have the benefit of parking in the front. Greg is flagged down by the neighbor.

"Can you hear that?" she says with contempt. "Its' past eleven o'clock."

"Yes Ma'am, I'll see what can do."

Greg is tall, almost seven feet. He is fit but he doesn't look like a roid cop. He is a Conch, born and raised in KW without pretensions. He enjoys his job and his family, especially his son, Junior, who just turned three and is a spitting image of him.

I'm the furthest from the door when the loud knock interrupts the dancing merriment. Kathy lets Greg inside. He is wearing his uniform and his custom-made cowboy boots.

"Ladies, there has been a complaint about the volume of the music, it's past …" he can't finish the sentence when I interrupt him.

"Dana you mofo; you got me a stripper!"

"No Cha Cha, I didn't hire a stripper!" Dana protested.

"No Ma'am," Greg is annoyed.

"He's on the skinny side but once I'm done, we'll feed him."

"No ma'am," Greg tries again.

"Stop ma'aming me and get over here," I insist.

"Ma'am, stop or I'll arrest you!"

"Oh yes you will," I say with delight.

I can't understand why the clothing doesn't snap off like the guy's in the movie '*Magic Mike.*' Dana tried to intervene, but nobody's going to interfere with my present.

"Hands off the merchandise; it's my present."

Silvia and Raúl come down to see what the ruckus is about. Halfway down the stairs, she recognizes Greg and in true police fashion jumps the rail and lands between me and the bemused trooper whose uniform shirt is down to his waist.

"He isn't a stripper," she scolds me. "This isn't your present. Now sit down over there while I explain this to my colleague."

My buzz is killed, instantly replaced with embarrassment and terror. Kathy, Anne, and Dana are doubled over with laughter. Raúl is sitting on the stairs hysterical.

"I'm so sorry about this," Silvia apologizes.

Greg starts laughing too. "You're not going to live this one down."

Key
West

Shorts

Birds of Paradise

Sarah was a crusty old whore who could pleasure a man top to bottom as good as anyone,
better actually, my fishermen buddies told me. I
met her in the Boca Chica Bar on Stock Island,
Key West's slummy neighbor, before they had to
install the metal detector at the entrance to keep
out the knives and guns.

Like Somerset Maugham (or was it Evelyn
Waugh?), I prefer sleazy bars to all others, and the
Boca Chica defined sleazy. It was the preferred
bar for Key West's fishermen and shrimpers and
the men and women chumming for them.

Men who'd been out fishing for weeks came
in so horny that any hole was a welcome port, and
from midnight on there was competition for their
dicks between whores and gay men. That's where
I met Sarah.

I'm a gay man who prefers straight men and
I pay them, which caused problems the night Sarah and I were on bar stools next to one another
and met for the first time in Boca Chica Bar. She
recognized me immediately as competition and
gave me a dirty look when I sat down. I tried to
disarm her by buying her a drink. That got me a

second, longer, but equally dirty look.

"Look, gay boy," (was I that obvious?) "thanks for the drink, but don't get in my way. I gotta do two of these jerks tonight to pay the rent, okay?" Her dentures clacked when she talked.

A degree in French Literature and three years in Les Halles, the Paris neighborhood with the most prostitutes, gave me a special tenderness for whores. How many had I swapped stories with—and comforted—in the café near my apartment there, the one I went to because it had heat and my apartment didn't?

"Deal, girl, but can I have your leftovers?"

Sarah laughed, and we started our friendship. What I didn't tell her was that I was exploring every slice of island life, trying to chronicle something that was authentic and now rare even here, something I knew was soon to disappear. These fishermen, these whores could never compete with the money gushing onto the island, turning it slowly into another rich man's playground. Houses that had sold for $20,000 when I'd moved here were now $1 million and up.

That night, Sarah and I swapped stories and checked out every man coming out of the john, wiping his nose. One man came out conjuring up an impressive bulge as he rubbed himself. Sarah and I looked at each other and laughed.

"Mine," she said and got off her stool and

walked over to the man.

I walked past them on the way to the john so I could overhear the transaction.

"Blow job," the man said.

"Twenty-five bucks," she said.

"Twenty."

"Deal. Teeth in or teeth out?" she asked.

"Out."

They walked outside.

Stuff like this anchored me to the island.

Sarah and I became friends those nights in the Boca Chica. She intrigued me as a person and as part of what made the island unique. I took her to lunch one Sunday at one of the restaurants on the harbor and was surprised when she showed up in a beautiful dress, instead of her usual slut clothes, and had her hair in a French bun.

We joked for a few minutes, then I scrutinized her as she watched the harbor traffic. I could tell that she had once been beautiful: cheekbones to slice meat on, lively eyes and strong jaws, the latter sunken into parody now with the loss of teeth. I also knew there was a story there, and I wanted to hear it.

The waiter came to take our order, and she ordered a steak.

"How would you like that cooked, ma'am?"

"Rare."

"Rare is bloody. Is that okay?"

"Look, knock the cow on its head, wipe its ass and bring me the steak, okay?"

The waiter was shocked. I laughed and ordered Eggs Benedict.

There were a few moments of silence after we'd placed the orders, and I didn't know how to break it. I decided finally on honesty.

"Sarah, I like you, I admire you, even, but I'm trying to write a story of the island as it's soon no longer going to be." I hesitated and thought for a minute. "I don't know how to say this, so I'm just going to say it. I think people like you and me are like one of those tribes about to become extinct in the world. The whole society around us is becoming all the same, and there isn't going to be room for us anymore. Am I making any sense?"

She looked out at the harbor—a beautiful, blue-hulled, double-masted sailboat was headed out—then looked back at me. She did that shifty, clicking thing with her mouth that people with bad dentures do.

"John, there's already no hope for anyone like me. I came here in '68 and had the choice of a $6//hour job heading shrimp, or $25 a pop giving up the pussy. I was out for fun, so guess which one I chose? It was different then, too. I was like a movie star back then when I walked into the Midget Bar or the Bucket of Blood on Caroline Street. Do you know what a salad girl is?" I shook my head.

"A salad girl is a woman the shrimpers hire to go out on the boat to cook the meals and do any of the men who want it. I see some of those boys today, married, and they have to look away from me because they're with their wives, and I was their salad girl. I understand that, but it hurts.

"Now I've got a tapped-out pussy, no teeth and no pension. We should have formed a whores' union back then," and she laughed, her dentures clicking again.

There was something noble in her unapologetic confession, and I admired her for it.

I decided out of affection not to probe any further.

I became her last resort friend, the one she called when she was broke and hungry, or worse, when she'd been beaten up and left on the side of the road somewhere on Stock Island.

One night I picked her up from the mangroves near the airport where two drunken tourists had gang-banged her then refused to pay after slapping her around. She called me from the airport's payphone, her voice carrying a kind of sadness I can't bear. I searched and found her, took her to my apartment and fed and comforted her. I showed her the black eye I'd just gotten from a straight boy who liked the blow job but then had to prove he 'wasn't like that' and got a weak laugh. I gave her a clean towel and led her to the shower. Why did we both seek dangerous sex? She did it for money—as I'd done to pay for a Master's degree in French—but there was something deeper, more animal, primal in our fucking. Society, to preserve a certain kind of order and progress, had channeled human sexuality into tunnels so narrow that some of us couldn't fit through. She and I didn't fit.

She came out of the shower, toweling herself. Ignoring the sunken mouth (where were the teeth? I didn't want to see those on the bathroom vanity during a nighttime piss break) one still saw a middle-aged woman of a certain beauty.

I poured us drinks, and we watched some stupid TV program. After the third drink, she leaned her head against my shoulder and I stroked it. We were friends, and that's what she whispered after a few minutes.

"I love you, gay boy."

"Love you, too, girlfriend."

I turned off the TV, put on Fleetwood Mac's Sara, and we cried a little on each other's shoulder.

The end was predictable. The Key West Citizen reported a jogger finding the body in Little Hamaca Park. Some customer had given her a hot shot. I walked out on my deck when I read the name and cried good-bye.

A fisherman with a soul organized a memorial at Stu's, the small coke-head bar on Stock Island and an overflow crowd showed up, spilling out onto the street. One shrimper waved everyone into silence and gave a surprisingly eloquent speech. "Farewell to a woman who gave the world pleasure," was his last line and he raised a glass. The crowd raised theirs, the music started and the dancing began.

"Good-bye, girlfriend," I whispered to the sky as I danced closer and closer to a drunken shrimper with a seriously cute ass. "This one's for you, girl."

Key West Shorts

Edgardo Alvarado-Vázquez

Three Tall Tales
That Include
Tennessee Williams

1 The Other Side of the Moon

"What's wrong with these people?" I was talking to myself, "Sure the play has problems but not that many!"

"Slow down! You're going to give me apoplexy!" I didn't notice how fast I was walking. The diminutive figure in sensible heels and cocktail dress was Audrey, my agent, charging on to keep up with my stride.

"You're taking this way too hard; we're only in rehearsals; the notices aren't out yet." She grabbed my arm and pulled back hard. "Jeez, slow down. Let me catch my breath."

"Audrey, didn't you see Walter Kerr walking out in the middle of the last act?"

"That's only one critic; did anybody else leave early?" She was still holding my arm.

Her breathing was still short when her eyes caught a glimpse of a figure across the street; she leaned on me and whispered:

"I think that is …"

I spun around and rushed up to 'the Lady.' I told her about my play and invited her to the opening night. She declined it with grace: "How wonderful. Thank you; I don't go out anymore."

She returned to her walk. I was mesmerized; Audrey gently jerked my arm again. "Let's go." After the play opened, my agent read me the notices. They were good for the actress and very bad for the play. I remember one in particular titled: *Bad Play Well-Acted.* I said to Audrey: "Two can play this game. If they're going to hate me, I will pay them back."

"What are you going to do?" Audrey looked at me as I winked.

"I'll throw a 'Bad Notice Party.'"

"Really," she said.

I rented the small ballroom at the hotel where we were staying and had it decorated with placards with some of the quotes from the notices. They were placed strategically throughout the room. A full bar was stocked and a small notice was placed on it: "All proceeds from your donations will benefit the ill children at St. Mary's Children's in Queens."

"I'm impressed," Audrey said. "You're going to make them pay for their own drinks?" She was wearing a blue moiré dress with open shoulders.

"Hell hath no fury like a queen scorned," I responded.

The actors were invited and warned that it wasn't a happy celebration. I arranged for some other friends to take my mother, who had invited herself to the opening night, for a fancy dinner at Lindy's, Broadway and 51st St. I'd send a note, with accompanying handsome tip, to the chef to come to the table, chat mother up, and offer her a couple glasses of sherry. She doesn't drink but will be obliged to the chef, being a well-raised southerner. I hoped that by the second glass, my friends would take her back to her hotel room happy and groggy. Mother didn't need to witness my vengeful side; she knew it well.

The ballroom could hardly hold the guests. I didn't know my lead actress knew 'the Lady' to whom I'd so boldly spoken a few nights ago on 42nd St. She made a terrific impression. True, the lovely face had aged but the beauty was still there; and also, the terrible shyness. She was worried, maybe by the number of people, but gracious. We chatted for a few minutes and discussed the play.

"I don't venture out anymore," her sensual purr could've killed me right then and there. "But I couldn't be excused from my dear friend's opening. I've made a couple of suggestions to her; you two can discuss them later."

The beautiful scene was destroyed by the voice of 'the director,' who was on cue according to our plans.

"Why don't you show us how 'it' is done using your most cherished character?"

He motioned with his hand and the table closest to me was cleared and moved aside. I draped the tablecloth around my head and body; the only thing visible was my face, my hand and my cigarette holder.

"*Ay, Ay,*" *I wailed.* "*Flores para los muertos,*"
"*Ay, Ay, Coronas para los muertos.*"

I went around the makeshift stage to the delight of all the guests. In the same tone, I read and 'wept' over all the bad notices and scolded each of the critics who dared to show up. I took particular interest in Walter Kerr of the *New York Times.* He took it like a champ. It was marvelous.

I looked around to find the eyes of 'the Lady.' She was having a splendid time and when I approached her, she said, "Thank you for a wonderful time." She turned to her friend, "Shall we?" My lead actress escorted her to the door and both departed.

The opposite door of the ballroom opened to welcome my lead actor; I wasn't expecting him. Despite my exhausted state, dealing with the on-going show for the critics, my night owl eyes landed on one of the most beautiful male specimens I'd seen in a while. He came in wearing the undershirt, disguised by a leather jacket, and the dungarees set aside for the play. I was still capable of falling in love at the time. And, despite my condition, (which was verging on mental and physical collapse) I was mad about the boy, but refrained from declaring it, as he was involved in my work. He was just about the best-looking boy I'd ever seen, with one or two exceptions, but I've never played around with actors; it was a point of morality with me until tonight. We were at a table in the back; his arm was around my shoulders. Audrey approached us.

"Are you really happy?" she asked.

I looked surprised. "Of course I am."

"Are you completely fulfilled young man?"

"Completely," I said. "Why do you ask me?"

"I just wanted to hear you say it." Audrey exaggerated a curtsey and walked away.

"This party is really swell," said the young actor. "Come, I've something to show you."

Down a couple of storeys by the stairs, I was in front of a shining, new black Indian Chief, not known to me, but the best example of motorcycle technology of the day. The actor was grinning and I was non-plussed. I was trying to be cute and asked him while I stroked the seat; "Italian leather?" He was puzzled. "Leather, who cares where it came from?"

"Well, can we ride it?"

He was already on top of it, "Hop on."

Here at the nadir of my despair, when my latest play had flopped, the most beautiful beast and I sped around Manhattan feeling an exhilarating surge of power between our thighs. I was enjoying the ride beside the East River, clamping his buttocks between my knees as we flew along the river drive with the cold wind whistling and a gorgeous moon above us. I clasped my arms around his chest. He didn't flinch. The motor was humming underneath us. I slid my hand inside his jacket and cupped his left breast. The motorcycle jerked a bit and resumed roaring. I closed my eyes and leaned my right cheek on his back. The river smelled of oil, brilliantine and musk. I was humming "heaven, I'm in heaven …" when the machine stopped. I was shaken from my musings when he got off the motorcycle, offered his hand and said. "Come on; time to see the other side of the moon."

2 The Bishop's Ring

At the end of the season in 1948, I remember calling Truman the night before we sailed to offer my car to pick him up.

"Tennessee, we will have a wonderful time!" and we did.

Truman Capote returned with me to the United States from England on the Queen Mary. It was a hilariously funny crossing. In those days, Truman was about the best companion you could want. He had not turned bitchy yet. Well, he had not turned maliciously bitchy. He was a gorgeous specimen, skinny and blond, with attractive brown eyes that drooped at the edges. He was full of fantasies and mischief. We used to go along the first class corridors of the Mary and pick up the gentlemen's shoes, set outside their staterooms for shining, and we would mix them all up, set them doors away from their proper places. The porter decided to catch the impish perpetrator, but we were faster, and he never caught us.

We had left Southampton when Truman began to notice that a portly and bibulous bishop was popping up unexpectedly almost everywhere Truman went. I began to notice him too. We would sit down at a bar on the ship when in would come the bishop, less steadily than the calm ocean and the seaworthy vessel could possibly account for. He would cast a glazed and anxious look about the bar. Then his eyes would light up as he spotted little Truman crouching before the bar, hoping to escape the attention of this eminent churchman. Gloom would disappear from his round face, and he would fairly plunge, quite uninvited needless to say, at the nearest bar stool, close to those occupied by Truman and me. He would order a glass of sherry and start his assault on poor Truman.

"Mr. Capote, are you a church-going gentleman?" started the conversation.

"No, your eminence. I haven't attended church since I came of age. I don't ascribe myself to any particular religion."

"Did your mother attend church? She must have!" said the bishop, slurring his words, continuing the interrogation.

Truman answered a little annoyed. "My poor mother was a southern Baptist, but I reject the visions of fire and brimstone that the bully pulpit was trying to impress on my young mind. I consider myself a free-spirited person."

"Well the Episcopalian church is not all about fire and brimstone. You should try it; I would love to guide you on your new-found journey."

"I bet you do, probably in your stateroom," Truman riposted. The bishop giggled.

"If that is where you want to start, I am not opposed to it."

"Not tonight, your eminence. I have a pounding headache, and tomorrow night I intend to wash my hair. One cannot disregard one's appearance. I learned that in the Baptist church." Truman rolled his eyes at me.

"You're a funny gentleman, Mr. Capote. I would like to pick your brain, maybe another day. You can't fault me for trying. Jesus was nothing but persistent about his job with the masses." The bishop sipped from his glass. I bet that wasn't his first sherry of the day or the evening for that matter. The bishop slowly raised himself from his chair and patted Truman on the shoulder, who cringed at the touch and moved slightly to avoid any other attempt from the reprehensible drunkard.

A dreadful confrontation between the bishop and Truman was unmistakably impending. Down it came like a bolt from heaven the next evening.

Truman and I were seated vis-à-vis at a table for two in the dining salon. With apparitional abruptness, the bishop had drawn up a chair between us and started his diatribe. His motive was not of an evangelistic nature. I mean not in the usual sense. Truman had declared himself quite uninterested in any church of any denomination.

The waiter brought forth the bishop's sherry. He didn't have to order it. Truman was uncomfortable.

"Good evening, gentlemen. Mr. Capote, shall we continue our conversation?" The chair groaned its disapproval of the rotund assault perpetrated on it by the bishop.

"If I remember my Sunday school correctly, it does not say anything about Jesus' childhood which may account for the lack of proper manners demonstrated by his representatives." Truman addressed me since the bishop seemed to have forgotten my presence at the table.

"We must carry God's teachings forward regardless, my child." The bishop took another sip from his sherry.

Truman began to stare at the bishop's massive ring.

"You know," he drawled sweetly to the bishop, "I've always wanted a bishop's ring." The bishop chuckled indulgently.

"A bishop's ring is only available to a bishop," was his answer.

"Oh, I don't know," countered Truman. "It occurred to me that maybe I might find one in a pawnshop, you know, one that had been hocked by a defrocked bishop."

He drawled out "defrocked bishop" in a way that left no doubt of his implication. The bishop turned redder than usual and excused himself from the table. We were not disturbed by his persistent approaches for the rest of the voyage.

At the end of the trip, I arranged, unbeknownst to our porter, a little "end of the crossing" party, in my cabin, to thank some of the staff that had taken care of Truman and me. I was particularly interested in an Italian waiter with whom I had exchanged a couple of complicit glances. Truman, aware of the situation, played the coy naïve southern deb he always wanted to be but couldn't. He tried to get in between my entertainment and me. Somewhere I heard a song that says that no one gets between me and my sister, but God save the sister who tries to come between me and my man; or something like that.

"Maximiliano!" Truman said in his most fake southern drawl. "So many consonants in your given name. Are there other strings of consonants in the rest of your name?" He continued.

Poor Max, as he was known on the ship, didn't speak any English, so he just smiled and nodded. I was having none of it, so I had to get Truman out of the room and presto. I got him close to the cabin door, pushed and locked it behind his exit to the delight of the rest of the guests. I was afraid of his vengeance; I thought he would disclose the "party" to the porter. But he had other plans. Later, after I achieved my purpose, he came into the stateroom and stole all of our clothing as we had fallen into the blissful slumber of pleasure.

The next morning, Max was frantic and forced to come down to his own quarters in his underwear. He gave his own porter the story of a French mademoiselle in need of care, which the porter swallowed whole and congratulated him on. I found this out as we disembarked in New York.

I said to Truman, "That was a pitiful revenge. Next time try harder."

"I'll get you and your little dog too!" he reposted, quoting the *Wizard of Oz*. He was foiled and he knew it. He took it in good jest.

Other evidence of our adventures during that crossing should be left to others to dissect, but suffice it to say that I have fond memories of the trip. When we later had our falling out, I still cherished these mementos of youth, debauchery, vitality, and happiness.

3 The Receiving Line

"Tenn," Thorton droned on as if he was delivering a homily during high Mass. "I liked your play but it is based upon a fatally mistaken premise. No female who had ever called herself a lady could possibly marry a vulgarian such as your lead character."

"And why not?" I replied. "Bad things do happen to good people as you've so well proven in your writings." Thorton thought about it for a few minutes. I was looking around the room where we were. It was sparsely furnished, almost monk-like: only two chairs, books in piles everywhere. Each pile had an open book at the top: English, Spanish, French and Italian. I picked up a well-worn copy of Sartre. The penciled annotations denoted a close reading. In a lonely corner, a typewriter sat on a small table covered by more papers. The single bed was almost hidden by other piles and papers. I thought about extending my hand and touching him—he seemed so lonely—but just for a minute and I shook that thought away.

We argued about the play for what seemed like an eternity. He would not give up his premise and I was exhausted. We parted and I didn't see him for a long time. I thought, privately, this poor guy has never had a good lay.

A few years later, during the Kennedy administration, writers, artists, musicians and politicians were invited to a banquet at the White House in honor of André Malraux. When my invitation arrived via post office, I called back the RSVP telephone number and kindly explained to the lady who answered that I wasn't going to be in Washington DC that weekend and put the affair out of my mind. A few hours later, the phone rang again, shaking me away from the work at hand. Annoyed, I answered the phone with a curt, "Yes?"

"Is this Mr. Williams? This is Letitia Balridge, social secretary for Mrs. Jacqueline Kennedy. She would like to speak to you." I dropped my lighted cigarette, almost setting the rug on fire.

"Mr. Williams," said the velvety voice with just a hint of a French accent. "My secretary just informed me that you declined our invitation to the White House. Is there anything that I can do to persuade you to change your mind?"

"Ah...ah," was all that came out of my throat.

"Mr. Williams?"

"Yes, Mrs. Kennedy. I'm sorry to sound a little bit surprised," I explained. "Of course, I can rearrange my appointments to accommodate your gracious invitation."

"I am so glad to hear that, Mr. Williams. Should I send a car for you at your hotel?"

"No, I will organize my own transportation.

Thank you for the offer."

"Well, that is settled. Thank you, Mr. Williams, I am looking forward to meeting you."

"I will be honored." I stood there for a few minutes looking at the phone.

The night of the reception, I had a seconal and a scotch as I put on my tuxedo.

"I look like shit," I said out loud as I creased my lapels into submission.

At the White House, all of us were told to line up in alphabetical order in a huge room walled with glittering mirrors. We were more or less lined up. The President and Jackie were about to appear. And here was Thornton Wilder bustling about like a self-appointed field marshal, seeing that we were arranged in our proper alphabetical order. I was engaged in conversation with Miss Shelley Winters as both of us were 'Ws.'

Wilder rushed up to me with the radiant smile of a mortician and shrieked, "Mr. Williams, you're a bit out of place, you come behind me."

I was just drunk enough to say to him, "If I am behind you it's the first and last time in my life." Wilder wasn't pleased, gave me a dirty look and got into place.

When the long alphabetical line moved slowly toward the President and First Lady, it was a magical moment. Mrs. Kennedy was wearing a strapless shantung by Christian Dior in a warm shade of pink. The mirrors in the room reflected every single angle, and she was eye-catching from every direction. The back was fitted at the top and had a series of bows that flared from the waist in a cascade of fabric, creating a slight train. She wore diamond earrings and white gloves that reached above the elbow. In her upswept hair she had fastened a jeweled ornament like a tiara. She looked like royalty. But I could not get my eyes away from the president, the most powerful man in the world and I was going to shake his hand. He was slightly taller than me and his tux was fitted enough to reveal his physique. I just marveled at him.

Miss Winters leaned on me and whispered, "You can look all you want, but I can get into that tux before you can even come close to the zipper." A quasi hysterical laugh came out of my mouth when the gloved small hand touched mine and her silky voice said; "I am so glad you could make it, Mr. Williams. After dinner I would like to hear your ideas about writing and the state of the theater in the United States."

"Enchanté," I replied.

The hand of the president came next, and my knees almost buckled. I don't even remember what he said. After dinner, we were escorted into the East Room, where violinist Isaac Stern, cellist Leonard Rose, and pianist Eugene Istomin played the Schubert Trio in B Flat Major. We were allowed to choose our own seating and Gore Vidal sat beside me. The son of a bitch looked resplendent in his tux.

"I couldn't help but notice that you almost melted in front of the president," he said with an impish smile.

"Wrong," I quipped, "I was composed and in full control of my faculties. But I couldn't get my eyes off his beautiful round derriere. It's very attractive."

Later Mrs. Kennedy assembled a group of us around her: Archibald MacLeish, Thornton Wilder, and Saul Bellow. Also gathered around her were dramatist Paddy Chayefsky, filmmaker Elia Kazan, playwright S. N. Behrman, and choreographer George Balanchine. I looked to my left and Gore Vidal winked at me and leaned toward the President to whisper something in his ear. Mr. Kennedy turned toward me and smiled.

As I was getting back into the car that was going to take me back to my hotel, Vidal rushed toward me.

"After I relayed your compliment to the president, he replied 'that is very exciting.'"

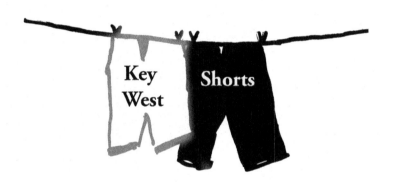

Key West Shorts

As the End Draws Near

He finished shaving, then stared at himself in the mirror, looking at time's erosion: the turkey wattle under his chin, the sagging jowls, the bags under his eyes. He had once been handsome enough that men and women, both, had thrown themselves at him. Now, when he walked into a bar, he was as invisible as old men and women had been to him when he was young.

He walked out of the bathroom into his bedroom where he kept a journal on the bedside table. It was something he used mostly for the construction business he'd retired from six months ago: (electricians on Fleming Street, Thursday; roofers on Shark Key, Monday), but also to capture thoughts he didn't want to lose.

He sat on the bed, picked up the pen and paused to compose his thought:

'Growing old' he wrote 'is like arriving in a foreign country where you don't speak the language and don't know the local customs.'

He read what he'd written to see if it satisfied him. He liked it.

He was seventy-one now, and it was a foreign country.

He put the journal down, got dressed and drove to Sandy's Café on White Street for a café con leche and Cuban toast. It had been a habit when he was still running his construction business and one of the pleasures of living in Key West. It was there that you met all the other construction workers getting coffee and got the best gossip on the island (did you hear that Esmeralda caught Jorge—her husband, a Cuban mason—trying on her clothes?) It was one of the things that made island living special.

When he showed up now, the other men greeted him warmly, but the conversation lacked spice; he had no construction gossip to share. He wasn't in the business anymore, and economically irrelevant. They patted him on the back in a caring though condescending way that saddened him, the kind of pat you give old people to reassure them.

Driving back on the familiar island streets, he felt even more dislocated. Was it that house or that one he'd renovated? And what was the name of the couple he'd done the one for on Southard where the wife wanted the electrical outlet above the bed-side table for her dildo? How unfair to start losing memory. The cruelest loss was the education he'd paid a slave's price to get. How do you lose the name of a poem and the author that had changed your life?

Back at home, he put on Ravi Shankar. What a beautiful arrow through Western brains that had been at Woodstock!

He pulled book after book from his shelves, seeking something that would take him back 'there' or out of here. He didn't find one.

What did it all mean, then, that effort to become educated, to learn French, to become a building contractor when it ended in front of a mirror that gave back no answers, only old-age reflections?

He sought understanding of this new life situation, but where would that understanding come from? In the past he could withdraw and self-examine, and his mind scoured everywhere and everything and illumined the next step: exile in Toronto, then Paris, then Key West. Where was the mental mechanism that had done that with such accuracy? Where was it now? He felt abandoned by his own mind. Was this the worst part of old age's punishment, or were there others worse to come? A low-grade dread began to suffuse his life.

One morning he wrote in his journal: How do you make the transition from living life constantly asking 'What does it all mean?' to this now: 'What did it all mean?'

Freed from the burden of running a construction business, he began to notice in depth things he'd only had time to glance at before. He began to walk more and ride his bicycle rather than use the truck. The slowness of both let him see the town with a fresh—or at least more attentive—eye. Old Town Key West, outside the tackiness of Duval Street, was still a beautiful mix of architecture and tropical vegetation.

Satisfying as it was to do that, there was a strangeness here, too: he now felt like a tourist in a town he had lived in for forty years. He no longer owned a house here, nor a business, and it was rare to run into anyone he knew on his walks, the opposite of what he'd experienced in his first years on the island.

He examined that closely and realized that the camaraderie of his construction buddies had shielded him from the transformation of the island's population. 90% of the people he'd met when he'd first arrived on the island in 1976 had left or were dead. He pulled out his address book one evening that confirmed it as he turned page after page with its strike marks or changes to Northern addresses.

He made a point of walking the AIDS Memorial on White Street Pier once a year. It was frightening and humbling to slowly read the names of over one hundred people he'd dined and worked with and for.

What do the years lived before count to me now, he thought in front of the mirror another morning? If I live only in my memories, I will be as sad as those soldiers who never rise above the one battle. Shouldn't a life lived honestly grant some grace in old age?

This was what he was thinking every evening when he uncorked the first bottle of wine and scoured his brain for a few true words, begging for just one lyrical phrase he could put in his journal that he could read the next morning with pleasure. He was craving to write, but couldn't focus the itch. A few lines, lyrical he hoped, about love found and lost? An essay about how his own beloved country had betrayed him?

One evening, well into a third bottle of wine, he fell to the floor, crawling around the coffee table imploring . . . whom? what? "One more Paris, one more Rimbaud or Baudelaire, one more person to love and sleep next to."

No answer came.

Sobbing, drunk, he fell asleep on the floor.

Key
West

Shorts

Nurse Irma

The silence was broken by gunfire, the rumbling of boats coming and going, and screams. The electricity went out first, and the generators kicked in for two days, given the amount of fuel in them. Then the water shut off, and by the fourth day they were running out of food. They used the back stairs to raid the cafeteria. They made two forays: Dr. Luis González, the orderlies, and two nurses who knew exactly where to look in the darkened space. By the third raid, they came back empty handed. Everything that wasn't bolted to the wall or too heavy to move was gone in the two surges that flooded the island; the first from the Atlantic, the second from the Gulf. The hospital was cut off, and became a tomb. Just before the hurricane hit, Dr. Dubois organized all the patients on the second and third floors of the hospital.

Today, when the looters, who were just hungry, tried to target the hospital, the first floor was abandoned and all possible access to the upper floors was barricaded.

Dr. González came running with the orderlies, John and Dan. They looked like a tag football team barreling down the hall.

"Dr. Dubois," said González as he stopped Dubois on the hallway. "They are forcing the elevator doors to gain access. Let's throw some furniture down the chutes. That'll keep them down there."

"What if you hurt someone Luis?"

"It's them or us, and I'm betting on our side," González stated.

"Okay, go ahead."

Luis entered into war-fighting mode. He was back in Rwanda and Zaire. He shut down his emotions; he retreated to the back of his brain, the levees of his mind breached. He came back to the second floor. He had just enough time to breathe and get his thoughts together when he found Dr. Dubois doing rounds. They were on no particular schedule. Just checking on the patients non-stop.

"James, when you hired me three years ago, you knew that I was returning to this country because of my experiences in Africa. I specifically told you I was leaving that behind and didn't want to visit those memories under any circumstances whatsoever," said an exasperated Dr. González. Lanky and taller than average, he had this habit of stooping down a little when talking to people who were shorter. Even though he was only thirty-nine years old, his experiences in Africa had taken their toll on his features; he seemed much older.

"Yes, yes," replied Dr. Dubois sighing. "This situation isn't my choice, but..." he couldn't finish his sentence.

"It is!" screamed Luis. A face peeked out of one of the rooms, checking on the argument.

"You and I both advised corporate of an evacuation plan, and if they hadn't been pushing pencils up their asses we would've evacuated and not been in the middle of this mess." He couldn't control his anger and frustration any longer.

"Luis, get a hold of yourself, the staff..." Dubois tried to say but was interrupted.

"I don't give a rat's ass who's hearing me. We've been in here for days and what you're trying to propose right now is completely and utterly unacceptable. This isn't the Himalayas or the Congo. This is Key West in the United States for God's sake. Where are the helicopters, where is the National Guard? I can't believe this is happening in the 21st century." Resentment distorted his face.

James Dubois, the picture of southern gentility, is mild mannered, manicured, and the product of a well-established career in hospital care and administration. He is the senior physician.

Dubois was speechless for a second, enough time for González to melt down into his chair, fists clenched by his temples.

"And whose bright idea was it to leave the youngest and most inexperienced administrator in the state of Florida in charge of this hospital? What is his name?" González calmed down a bit.

"Jason Phillips, he volunteered," Dubois responded.

"Did you notice he hasn't left his office?"

"The less he knows, the better for us," Dubois sighed. "The less he has to report to corporate. It's a legal safety measure. We discussed it."

Some patients had died during the storm. The circumstances were recorded, their bodies put in the morgue, and the family members stayed on the second floor. There was nowhere else to go. The staff was discussing something in hushed tones among themselves.

Margarita Céspedes del Rio, in her nineties, was the last member of one of the most distinguished Cuban families of Key West. The years of smoking Pall Mall unfiltered cigarettes had caught up with her. She's been attached to a breathing machine since last year when one of her lungs collapsed. Margarita complained about everything.

"I'm entitled to voice my opinions," she decreed. She complained about the nurses, the doctors, the orderlies. About her bedsores, the constant pain and the inconvenience of being inconvenienced.

"I'm telling you, it's a conspiracy to kill me," she screamed to the nurse. "You all want my money."

The nurses decided to put her in a single room, even under these circumstances, for the benefit of everybody else.

"Esto no se hubiera visto en Cuba," she spitted in Spanish.

"In Cuba, the way things are now," Nurse Pat Menardi, head of the skeleton nursing staff, turned on her shoes and shot a sideways look at Margarita, "Raúl Castro would've fed you to the pigs, since Fidel died; he," she stressed the pronoun, "would've executed you in the baseball arena. And when was the last time that you were in Havana? In the fifties? You've no idea what you're talking about. I need to find Dr. González."

Menardi found González in the third floor checking on patients.

"The nurses and orderlies are looking for answers, doctor." She had evacuated her family and stayed behind. She couldn't leave the hospital. It was her duty as a nurse and as a Christian soldier. She always found solace in God's grace.

"They want to know if someone is coming. And if not, what the plan is."

"I won't even discuss the matter," answered González. "I will not take responsibility. Go and ask Dubois if you want, and please—leave me out of it. That's the end of the matter. Now I'll do rounds." He turned without waiting for a reply.

Not far away, Menardi found Dr. Dubois. "My nurses want to know what the plan is. Yes or no. Are we helping these people out of their misery?"

"Yes," James muttered under his breath before walking away from her.

Night came. The staff was working non-stop. Whoever could sleep did so restlessly. Three more patients died.

The next morning, the senior staff gathered on the third floor in front of Jason Phillips' office. He was a bachelor, well regarded by the company. He didn't interfere with what was happening around him.

"I'm not going to tell you what to do," he said, visibly unhappy with being thrown in the middle of the argument. "I've never been in a hurricane before. Neither the company nor any of us foresaw this situation. As you might've noticed, I have stayed in my office during this whole ordeal. I believe each of you is a hero, that each one of you has worked and is working under the worst possible circumstances and that's what I'll tell corporate. I really believe that, and this is the extent of my involvement." He turned around and went back into his office and locked the door.

The discussion about what to do with the patients in crisis went on for what seemed forever. It was around four a.m. according to the wall clock. Luis remained seated, hands holding his temples. Finally, Nurse Menardi said: "Would anyone join me in prayer?" A circle formed; Dr. González stayed seated.

"Lord, I raise my hands in praise and glory.
You granted us hands so we could heal,
so we could reassure and pass on serenity.
Our hardship is the pathway to your grace;
grant us the courage to serve
and to make the best decisions possible
in this day that our government has failed us
and our strength has abandoned us.
Guide us, let us be your vessels,
shine your divine light on us."

Menardi shook a bit and exhaled. She was transformed by the spirit. Dr. Dubois then produced a handful of syringes. Nurse Menardi said, "These syringes contain a palliative. The dosage has been doubled. It's enough. I'm going to give them to you. If anybody is worried, I'm taking full responsibility. God gave me permission. I'm at peace. You don't have to do this if you're uncomfortable. If you have questions about the priority list, ask me. If you need me, I'm going to be in Margarita's room."

Luis stood up and picked up his medical bag.

"I'm leaving," he said, "maybe someone needs me outside." He paused for a moment, looked at his bag, dropped it, and started to walk out.

Dubois stopped him and whispered in his ear. "Luis, please, don't be too harsh in your judgment of me."

Menardi made her way to Margarita's room.

"Are you coming to kill me?" Margarita asked.

"No Margarita, I'm here to give you your sedative."

"The pain is killing me, this hospital is killing me." Margarita made a fist with her hand and tried to hit the side of her respirator machine. *"Esta máquina de mierda no funciona!"*

"Margarita, the hospital is out of power. You know that don't you? That's why the respirator isn't working." Menardi took her arm. It was so thin that she could put her hand around it. The skin was paper-thin; she could see every vein, every capillary, every frigile bone. She wrapped the rubber tube gently, and Margarita tried to jerk her arm from her.

"Hush, let me do this," Menardi said. Margarita gave in.

Margarita sighed, relieved. Somehow she knew. Menardi opened the top drawer of the side table, there she found a brush; it had a silver handle and bristles made of horsehair. She cupped

Margarita's head very kindly and started combing her long white hair.

"¿*Tata Nana?*" Margarita was far away, child-like.

"*Sí, mi niña.*"

"*Te he estado esperando por mucho tiempo.*"

"Yes dear my dear child, I know. I have been waiting to see you too." Menardi, brushing her hair, started saying the Lord's Prayer. She lost track of time. It was over. She looked at her watch and noted the time in Margarita's chart. Dan's head appeared at the door. Menardi nodded. He came in with John and the stretcher; they placed her on it without effort and covered her with a sheet. Dubois was coming down the hallway and stumbled upon them. He looked at Menardi and crossed himself.

Dr. González made his way through the same door that accessed the cafeteria. It took him some time. He walked into something, stopped, and grabbed it. He caught the leg of a metal chair, lifted it and threw it aside. He stumbled and fell in a puddle of water. He stood again brushing his hands against his wet clothing. He pushed around discarded furniture and equipment that had been rearranged by the wind and the receding water.

He ended up at the back entrance of the hospital. At the crack of dawn, he could discern part of the ambulance ramp. It led to water. The pungent smell of oil combined with God-only-knew-what, made him cover his nose with his hand. "Damn!"

Nurse Menardi went back to Margarita's room, stripped down the bed and started putting her things in one of the bags that the hospital provides for outgoing patients. She looked at the brush, one more time. "I know you're happy now; there's no more pain," she was standing near the window. Day was breaking. A noise, a very faint whap, whap, whap, whap; Menardi leaned on the windowsill, trying to see what was happening? Where was it coming from?

"Oh my God!" she said out loud and ran to the hallway. "Dan, John, get over here stat."

Light started streaming slowly, peeking through the clouds. Dr. González looked at his watch. It was broken. Noise started rising from the smelly waters and wind started whirling around him. The whap, whap, whap, whap, startled him. He ducked instinctively, hands on his head. It wasn't gunfire. It was a rotor blade. The light from the helicopter blinded him. Now he distinguished the sound of a motorboat approaching from the west side of the ramp. He could see the orange and blue stripes and the iconic logo.

A strained voice came from the reeking waters enhanced by a megaphone. "Stay where you are, place your hands on your head. This is the United States Coast Guard."

Wesley Sizemore

A Road Not Traveled

It happens most often when I am stopped at a traffic light. There I am, looking up at the signal, but I am somewhere else. I am somewhere in the past again. My wife nudges me, or gently urges me to go when the light turns green and occasionally asks if I am all right. We are at that age where we watch each other for the early signs of mental decline, that decline, the one all old people dread.

We have had an enviable marriage, my wife and I. We are still each other's best and closest friends. I would not give up the comfort of cuddling up to her back at night for a king's ransom.

But what I am thinking about, in those lost moments at traffic lights, fills me with a sense of loss I do not understand hitting me again this hard, at this time in my life, and don't yet know how to share with her. Has our move to Key West somehow triggered dormant memories?

And why have I kept it to myself all this time?

I was a Sophomore at the University of Missouri, living in a room with kitchen privileges, one of thousands of lower-middle-class boys and girls climbing up the next step in society. I shared the off-campus house with men studying Agriculture or Engineering. I was studying languages, probably the only person on a campus of 20,000 in that program who was putting himself through college.

I inspected Coca-Cola bottles on weekends, watching them as they passed in front of a light as they came out of the bottle-washing machine to see if anything: cockroaches, cigarette butts, or condoms had been left inside, pulling the offenders off the line. At night, I washed UPS trucks.

During the day, I was reading some of the most glorious literature in the world and having it put into context by men and women who were passionate about it. For me, this was education as I'd dreamed it to be, and it gave my weekend and night-time labor value.

Where I lived, the men, all as busy as I, because only poor boys lived in that house, asked me questions and looked at me when I answered them with, not disdain, exactly, but certainly incomprehension. A language major? They didn't make fun of me because I was the envy of the house for the women who came looking for me and who they suspected I was successful with. But why study languages? Where was the money in that?

One man in the house, Bill Thomas, was a short, muscular, good-looking Agriculture major who liked smoking cigars and laughed a lot. Bill owned a '57 Ford convertible that he kept in immaculate condition and which we all envied him for. When Bill asked me questions about my major and what I was studying, he listened with not just curiosity but interest.

To this day, I don't know exactly why we became friends, but we did. One day he asked me if I wanted to go out drinking with him and, surprised but pleased, I agreed. Sitting in a red-neck bar, listening to corny country-western music, we got drunk on cheap beer and realized we really did like one another. He was studying Agriculture to take over the family farm, but suspected, as did I, that there was a bigger world out there and we talked about seeing it someday with a naiveté I look back on that makes me want to go back in time and wrap our arms around each other like I did with my children, much later, when they were young, asleep.

Bill began loaning me his car for my dates, pumping me for details if I gave him the thumbs-up sign that I'd scored.

One morning, in early Spring 1966, fragrance and beginning warmth in the air, Bill asked me if I'd like to ride up to Moberly with him, a town two hours north. "One of the rear quarter panels on my car is rusting out and they have some junkers in a yard up there I can get one from. Come on, you're a brain, skip some classes, it's a nice day."

Off we went, top down, devil-may-care, swapping stories about some of the worst things we were doing to put ourselves through college. I told him about a German prof who thought he was doing me a favor by offering me a job at the university library for fifty cents an hour. Sixty hours a month there wouldn't even have paid my rent.

Bill laughed and told a similar story about a prof who offered him a job mucking out the college's stables paying a fourth of what he made welding part-time.

Then we were quiet for a while, sucking up springtime, looking at trees in early foliage and flowers sprouting in the right-of-way, once in a while joking about something stupid one of our housemates had done.

Bill found the junkyard in Moberly, found a '57 Ford that someone must have died in, judging by the damage to the front of the car, then asked for a welding torch. I stood in serious awe when he put on the welder's hood, lit and adjusted the torch, and cut out a rear quarter panel from the wrecked car. We loaded it in his trunk, then began the trip back, stopping at a liquor store to buy some beer, which shortly launched hilarious stories about our respective efforts at getting laid.

He'd had one conquest only, he told me, a woman who had scared him.

"I found out after we started doing it that she saved all the rubbers," he said. "She washed them out and dated them."

"Bill, come on, you're making that up."

"I swear to you. I backed out of there like a dog out a weasel's hole when she showed me." And we both started laughing. Then he confessed to me that the whole idea of marriage scared him. "How do you stay in love with someone your whole life? Yet I want a woman I can do that with. How do you find one like that?"

I was surprised at the turn of conversation, but honored, too.

"Bill, you'll find one, trust me. You're a good man. Just take your time."

I think he took comfort in hearing that from me if for no other reason than that I'd had more experience with women. Then I told him about my doubts at killing myself to get an education in something as financially impractical as languages.

"I wouldn't worry about it," he said. "You're smart, you'll figure something out. And you're studying something you say you really like."

Reluctant for the brief escape to end, we stopped at our redneck bar on the outskirts of

Columbia and began knocking back more beer, both 'high' from a Spring afternoon's escape from the drudgery we were both enduring to pay for our educations. The more we drank, the more we laughed. Bill went off to take a leak and when he came back we started spinning fantasies.

"Hey, man, why don't we just say fuck it and pool our money and take my car and drive out to California. If we run out of money we can stop along the way and work a few days."

"Yeah, let's do it. We could stop and see the Rockies and the Grand Canyon. Imagine seeing the Grand Canyon!"

"What if we could get a job on a freighter out of 'Frisco'?" he said. "Go see some of the world. Would you do it?"

"Hell yes."

And off we went, fueling our fantasy with more beer, embroidering all we would do on the trip until someone played Hank William's 'I'm So Lonesome I Could Cry' on the jukebox at the same time reality settled in on us and we fell quiet, accepting that the idea of a trip to California was fun but just fantasy. I had to wash trucks that night, he had to tend bar, we both had classes the next day and Vietnam hung over both of us.

Out of that afternoon, the friendship deepened and we were close from then on, my first friendship, actually, because the constant moving my father's Navy career had demanded precluded making friends in my youth, and the habit of not making friends had stayed with me.

Bill graduated, then was drafted right after, but came back to Columbia on his leaves to see Helen, the sweet woman he'd started dating. Helen was wonderful, funny in complicated ways I appreciated, and obviously in love. She and I hit it off from our first meeting.

They married right before Bill was shipped to Vietnam. I was his best man, and the hugs we gave each other before he got in the car to drive off to his honeymoon were heartfelt. "I love you, man," he told me and I told him back, this back before it was okay for men to say that and not be considered queer. A good man had found a good woman, and I was happy for them both.

"Stay safe, man," I told him. He grinned and looked back out the car window and gave me a 'thumbs up' as they drove off with the strings of tin cans rattling behind them.

He was killed in some unpronounceable place not three months after he was in Vietnam. Helen, sobbing, called me with the news. Watching that casket being lowered into the ground with Helen crying on my shoulder changed me forever. It was the first event in my life I was never the same after.

The lies the government had told and was still telling about the war convinced me to refuse induction and when my draft board (and the Supreme Court) refused to allow me to object to the war, I went to Canada and from there traveled the larger world Bill and I had talked about that Spring afternoon in that redneck bar.

The night I walked out of the Gare du Nord and saw the lights of Paris for the first time, I put down my backpack and knelt on the sidewalk to memorize the moment and whispered: "Bill, this is for both of us."

I returned to the United States only years later after Carter granted amnesty.

Apart from the incomparable friendship of a good marriage, I never made another friend, only friendly acquaintances, which seemed enough.

When I was close to retirement, the company I worked for sent me to Washington. I knew I had to go 'there,' to the huge black tombstone, but 'THERE' was a place I did not want to go to.

The taxi dropped me off, and I walked towards IT. Fifty or so people were there, many as old as I, some with children, and I approached with great fear, mega-death.

I looked away, at first, from the unbearable quantity of names, then finally turned and walked slowly down the years, hoping somehow THAT name would not be there, that it was a terrible mistake, and he was now a fat, happily married farmer with grandkids. We, senior citizens now, would call each other and visit once a year and reminisce, wives looking on indulgently.

No, the tombstone said. He's dead. Look here, HERE, this panel, 1968. That's his name— William Robert Thomas—he's dead.

I began to cry when I touched his name, my head against black granite. A woman walked over and, saying nothing, put her arm around my shoulders. Then she patted me on the back and left. I gained control of myself. "Bill, why did you have to go get killed," I asked the granite. "You were my only real friend and I've never stopped missing you."

Granite is as dead as the names inscribed on it. It can only record. It cannot explain.

So that is what I am thinking about all these decades later, waiting for the light to change. More and more, I ask myself why we didn't do it, say what the hell and drive to California. Would it have turned fate's path from fatal for him? I don't know. I only know that two young men, boys, sitting in a bar in Columbia, Missouri in 1968, spinning the fantasy of a trip, should have taken it.

The light changes. My wife puts her hand on my arm as I drive forward and in the touch there is both comfortable love and a subtle request for reassurance. I touch her back and give her a quick kiss, but I cannot yet share the sadness I feel because it might cause her to think I have regrets about my life with her and our marriage—which I have never had—and her latest surgery lifting off a breast has left her sad and vulnerable. Comforting her is an act of love that gives me ... what? Something more wonderful than I deserve.

But I do have this one, great, indigestible regret. You were a soul-mate, Bill. What if we had taken the trip? Would you still be alive? I still miss you.

The Jewish Conspiracy

He was born into Southern poverty, but then traveled the Western hemisphere when his father enlisted in the U.S. Navy to spare the family that impoverished existence. Apart from the confusing rants of those Southern fundamentalist preachers who praised the Israelites of the Old Testament and condemned the Jews of the New Testament, Alan didn't know anything about Jews or their religion apart from random readings in the Bible. Southern peasant—he—they were as invisible to his youthful radar as Hottentots or Guarani.

In high school, he saw a documentary about the Holocaust that horrified him: the mounds of bodies, the ovens, the starving survivors. That was his first glimpse into the evil that humans are so capable of, made so evident in the industrial century he'd been born into.

In college, Alan met a few men who said they were Jewish, but they didn't seem much different from himself, so he didn't give it much thought. He was working twenty hours a week and taking full course loads, so there wasn't much time to think about global issues, any issues, anyway.

The war in Vietnam transformed his life as it did the others of his generation, the ones it didn't put an end to. When it became evident that the war was going to affect his own life, Alan was angry. He was working to finish a Master's degree in American History and now had to confront this.

He began to pay attention and to weigh the government's pronouncements against the anti-war movement's protest information. Midwesterner by birth and disposition, it seemed inimical to his character not to believe the government. But the teach-ins, with the battle-scarred returning veterans telling what was really happening in Vietnam were compelling, and he was convinced.

He was inducted six weeks before finishing his M.A., after he'd written his draft board that he would perform the four years of alternative duty that Quakers and Jehovah witnesses were allowed. He had also written the Supreme Court, invoking the rights established after the Nuremburg trials, that an individual had a legal and moral right—and duty—to refuse what he believed to be an unjust or illegal order.

His draft board told him he had to report for induction. The Supreme Court told him that he had to object to ALL war, not just one, to qualify for exemption. How could someone exempt himself from all war if his own country was attacked?

He went to his induction in St. Louis, and when they refused again to let him perform alternative service, he walked out of the building, caught a bus to the St. Louis airport and bought a one-way ticket to Toronto. He landed in Toronto on the night of December 10, 1968, with light clothing, no contacts, and $1.75 in his pocket. It was the most traumatic event of his life, one that he honored each year on that night by turning off the phone, turning down all invitations to dinner, putting on the clothes he wore that night and reading his journal entries describing his feelings and the last American city lights he flew over in his escape.

When he'd landed in Toronto—a town he would have had minutes of difficulty locating on a globe a day before, he asked two de-planing passengers where the YMCA was and how did he get there. They were all helpful (aren't Canadians wonderful?) and showed him how to ride the subway and change stations.

He told the check-in clerk at the 'Y' that he was a war resister and didn't have enough money for the room he needed. The clerk laughed and told him he had a war resister room-mate and gave him a room out of the cold. "Pay us later. Go upstairs and get warm. Come back and pay for the room when you get settled."

It was the loneliest night of his life.

The Canadians were angels, and he survived, then prospered as he went to work in a restaurant and started work on a Master's in French literature at the University of Toronto.

A year and a half after his flight into exile, he saw a sign on a university bulletin board in April for a charter flight to Amsterdam that summer, summer of 1971, $150 Canadian round-trip. He borrowed money, bought the ticket, and took the train to Paris two days after landing in Amsterdam. Walking out of the Gare du Nord, that night, that summer, seeing those lights, he knew, somehow, his life was never going to be the same again. His ideas about food, architecture, public transportation, the role of government in a nation's life—everything—were about to be changed forever.

At the end of that summer, halfway through the return charter flight from Amsterdam to Toronto, the flight attendants came through the cabin distributing American customs and immigration forms. What was this? He stopped the woman and asked her about it. She explained that the 747s were so new that KLM didn't have many crews certified to fly them, so they were stopping in New York to pick up a qualified crew who was going to fly the plane to Toronto and then back to Amsterdam that night.

"Kennedy airport doesn't have international transit lounges, so every passenger who arrives has to clear U.S. Customs and Immigration. We'll be there an hour and a half at the most, then fly back out," she explained, like it was nothing.

He was gut shot and ran to the bathroom to throw up. He was probably the only American on a plane filled with Dutch and Canadians. He was going to be arrested and be sent to prison for more than four years. He had spent the first two years of his political exile crossing back into the U.S. with false ID papers, sending his draft board and the FBI postcards and photos, daring them to catch him: photo of himself standing in front of the Statue of Liberty, photo standing on the Capitol building's steps, postcard from the FBI's own headquarters—he'd taken the tour—and they really wanted him. They had visited all his relatives and had tapped his parents' and sister's phones.

Catching him by chance like this would start an FBI party.

He went back to his seat and called the flight attendant back and explained his situation. "You didn't tell us this plane was going to land in New York, so you have to protect me. Is a Dutch

flight crew really going to watch a war protest-
er dragged off to prison? One hundred thousand
Dutch showed up at the last anti-Vietnam protest in Amsterdam."

She went back to the cockpit, then came
back and said there was nothing they could do.

"Just let me stay on the plane while you
change crews. Come on, it's Dutch territory."

Back to the cockpit, return, shaking her head
'NO.'"Safety regulations. All passengers must de-
plane."

He started stripping his pockets of passport,
wallet, anything that could identify him. If they
were going to grab him, he wasn't going to make
it easy.

Then the man across the aisle coughed to
get his attention. "I'm sorry, but I couldn't help
over-hearing what you said to the flight attendant. Would you mind terribly telling me what's
going on?" Canadian English, Dutch accent.

He told him the whole story.

"Distressing, distressing," he said and turned
to his wife and told her, in Dutch, the problem.

When the man turned back, he explained
that he was Dutch and Jewish by birth, that he
and his wife had both lost their parents in the
Holocaust, and he was now a research chemist
for Shell Oil in Canada, and that he and his wife
housed another American war resister in their

home outside Toronto.

"Let me see what I can do," and he called the flight attendant back and hit her with a four-minute stream of forceful Dutch that obviously shook the woman, who walked back to the cockpit again.

"She looked upset. What did you say to her?"

"I told her that we Dutch have a centuries-old history of protecting political refugees, which you are, and that if this flight crew did not find a way to protect you, I would expose them to my editor friend at the Toronto Star, and my editor friend at De Telegraaf in Amsterdam, and that they would be shamed forever in front of all the Dutch and Canadians."

Alan started crying a little and Mr. Abrams reached across the aisle and patted him on the back. "You men are brave, trying to stop the world's most powerful country from fighting a war they shouldn't be fighting. Thank you for doing that."

A few minutes later, the pilot announced that "because of the large number of small children and babies on board, we have received special permission to use one of the KLM boarding lounges as a transit lounge. You will NOT have to pass through U.S. Customs and Immigration."

They landed and were escorted off the plane by armed guards to the lounge, where the doors were locked and attended by other guards. They were almost shoulder to shoulder, and dozens of small children and babies were squalling. Alan had never felt so guilty for causing pain. Every once in a while, Mr. Abrams would pat him on the back and nod encouragement. Two over-heated hours later, they were escorted back to the plane which took off and landed in Toronto an hour later.

Alan was crying again when he hugged and thanked Mr. and Mrs. Abrams in the Toronto airport and said good-bye. Midwestern boy had just been saved from four years of Federal prison by two Dutch Jews. How had he earned that?

***

Fast forward to amnesty, Midwestern boy's return to his treacherous motherland. Key West, he decided.

Years into renovating houses, he was doing one for a Jewish couple from New York. Halfway into the project, he was diagnosed with an angiosarcoma, cancerous tumor of a blood vessel, survival rate of fifteen per cent if they caught it early, and they hadn't.

He didn't tell Alice or her husband, making excuses for his absence from the job for the thirty-nine radiation treatments, the last ten leaving him with desperate fatigue.

Alice found out, smart New Yorker, and

grilled him the next time she saw him on the job.

"What? You're sick and trying to hide it from us. What a shmuck. Tell me everything."

He started giving her all the information even his mother didn't have and ended crying and she took him in her arms. "Come on, little goyim, you're tough. Besides, you can't die. You need to finish my house." He dried his eyes, they looked at each other and started laughing.

He didn't have health insurance, like ninety percent of the workers on the island, and the hospital and radiation center pursued him for two months, threatening locks on his bank account and seizure of assets. Then, suddenly, all the bills had been paid and the threats stopped. Alice had paid everything. When he called her to confirm it, she said: "Alan, when you came to me and gave me the kickback the cabinet guy gave you, I realized you were someone who would never survive in New York, and someone I will always trust, never mind the issue. And please don't cry again. Gets me all weak and slushy, and I have some New York lawyers I have to deal with in a few minutes. Love you kid. Come up and visit us."

***

Ten years later, Alan's first novel was published at the same time he was re-wiring a house for a Jewish couple from Maryland. The husband had a teasing brand of humor that matched his own and they hit it off, his wife rolling her eyes at the sarcastic jokes they lobbed back and forth. When the renovation was finished the couple gave a catered party for thirty people on their back deck. Some of the guests were the construction workers who'd worked on the house, and the others, the couple's friends from up North. When dessert had been served, the waiters began bringing out copies of his novel the husband had bought, one for each guest. When Alan saw what he'd done and started crying, the husband came over and put an arm around him and whispered in his ear: "Come on, author, you know that cockroaches don't cry," which made Alan laugh. One of their long-running jokes was to address each other by the name of a character in a novel. One day the husband had called Alan 'Samsa' which earned him a stern look: Samsa was Kafka's cockroach.

Alan laughed, got up to give thanks, and gave praise to a couple whose kindness was manifest, and began signing books.

That was the Jewish Conspiracy in his life.

Wesley Sizemore

Butterfly

When I turned sixty, while I still had some money and good health, I began to think about the last things I wanted to do in my life and hadn't, the Bucket List in the movie.

My personal list of things not experienced included seeing Khufu's Pyramid, Istanbul, and Venice. How could any human not want to see what our earlier versions had accomplished?

I checked those off one by one in difficult breaks from running my business. But as high on my list as seeing Khufu's Pyramid, or the Hagia Sophia, and St. Mark's and the canals was to see a live production of Puccini's Madama Butterfly.

Men and women who had lived in Key West in the '60s and '70s, even if they left for someplace else, carried the island in their soul and never lost the connection to their friends from back then. Meeting one of the displaced in Portland, Taos or Costa Rica required no transitory greetings: we were still dancing together in the Monster disco, and the conversations took up right where we'd left off. We loved one another and could say that without reserve.

"Remember that night when Tennessee..."

was one of the stories we always recounted.

Tennessee had been in line to get into the Monster disco where we all gathered on Sunday evening back then for the $1 spaghetti dinner and hot disco music. Tennessee, in the middle of the line, whispered something—we assumed a proposition—to the man in front of him and the man jerked away. Tennessee (Tom if you knew him like we did) whispered something again, and the man pushed Tom/Tennessee, who fell, and the man left the line mumbling: 'Weirdos.'

The man behind the most famous playwright in America reached down to give him a hand up, and when Tom stood back up and thanked the man, the man responded: "Sometimes, Mr. Williams, we have all depended on the kindness of strangers," and everyone in line recognized the line from Streetcar and applauded. Mr. Williams bowed a thank you, got as drunk as us and we all danced together.

An island friend of mine, Lupe Flores, had left Key West for Greenwich after he'd grown tired of running Gato Gordo, his Mexican restaurant. We had stayed in touch, swapping salacious stories—his, sometimes fictionalized—of our seduction of straight men.

One Sunday, *The New York Times* Entertainment Section listed the operas being performed that season. *Butterfly* was on the list. I bought two tickets, called Lupe immediately and invited him. "Tickets on me, dude, Kleenex on you." He laughed. Lupe was as emotionally soft as I was. Together we'd spent a king's ransom trying to help boys in trouble straighten out their lives and gotten our hearts broken in the attempt.

Lupe met me at La Guardia and we took a taxi to the non-descript Mid-town hotel I'd booked a room in. I changed clothes and we roamed the city in taxis—my treat. Lunch in the West Village, tour of the Egyptian exhibit at the Met and the Rothko exhibit at the Guggenheim, the most perfect melding of paintings and building I'd ever seen: paintings getting darker and darker as you circled downwards to the end, Rothko's end. Lupe and I left Wright's building silent.

The taxi let us out in front of Lincoln Center (whose architecture does not please me), and we joined the crowds filing in for one of the things I most admire humans for—strange animals—the ability to be moved by things as abstract as writing and music.

Lupe turned to me as we walked in. "I owe you, friend."

"Just listen and cry and you won't even owe me a café con leche." He laughed.

We found our very expensive seats (how many times do you get to see *Butterfly* in your life?) Lupe sat to my left, and a middle-aged couple seated themselves to my right, woman next to me: pleated dress, expensive and every pleat perfectly pressed, shoes perfectly shined, blouse starched into involuntary servitude, and hair, nails and makeup top class. I nodded to her and her 'friend' (no wedding rings) and received no return nod. 'Okay, bitch,' I thought to myself. 'Try those manners in Paris and see what it gets you.'

Was she here because her companion was trying to seduce her by showing her his appreciation of great art? Or was he here because she was trying to 'humanize' him as the French say.

Then the overture, and the curtain rising on a beautiful tea-house. Lupe and I grabbed each other's hand.

Lupe and I then grabbed hands again at the usual moments: when Pinkerton 'marries' her, when he leaves promising to come back for her.

We started crying at '*Un Bel Di.*' Most gay men of our age have experienced someone promising to come back 'some fine day.'

And then the tragedy: Pinkerton's ship has come back and Butterfly sees it in the harbor and sings a glorious welcome. She is so happy: he's come back for her as he'd promised. She and their son try to stay awake all night, waiting for

Pinkerton to walk up from the harbor, but they finally fall asleep.

Pinkerton arrives the next morning, but with his American wife to claim the son.

Cio-Cio-San's reaction is brilliant as she switches in a minute from being over-joyed—he's come back as he promised—to recognition of the reality: the American wife and the demand for the child.

She recovers her dignity and surrenders to the situation. She is, after all, just a geisha.

But. . .but. . .one of the most heart-rending pieces of art in all human history is Cio-Cio-San giving up her child, kneeling in front of him, holding him, asking that he never forget his mother's face.

And when Pinkerton and his wife leave with the child, Cio-Cio-San kills herself.

Lupe and I were leaning against each other crying.

The woman to my right didn't react even a millimeter to a woman giving up her child.

The audience stood at the end and gave the performers three encores. The woman next to me and her companion stood and applauded, tepidly.

When Lupe and I walked out and caught a taxi to the Village for a night of drinking and dancing, we talked in the ride about the couple.

"WASPs," he hypothesized. "Frozen since

the arrival of the Mayflower."

While dancing in the gay bar with a hundred other men and women, I gave a silent thank-you to Puccini and Cio-Cio-San and friendships like mine with Lupe. Why would any human being want to go through life un-moved by these works of art and friendships? Then I did a really cool move on the dance floor that surprised Lupe and we both laughed and did 'high fives.'

He left with another man and I left alone, happy to guard in my heart the jewel of Cio-Cio-San's sacrifice.

Lupe and I hugged and exchanged love greetings when we said good-bye the next day.

I played my recording of *Butterfly* my first night back on the island, crying again.

Lupe died two years later, another victim of the green monkey virus, and I lost another soul-mate. I drank myself into inebriation when I heard the news, put on '*Un Bel Di*,' walked out on my deck and screamed 'FUCK YOU, FUCK YOU' to what or whom?

Wesley Sizemore

The Lost Son

He stared at the bills in front of him and re-alized that among the many things he'd lost control of during his alcoholism were his finances. There was no way around it. He had to rent out one of the rooms in his house.

Alcohol had numbed the slashing pain of losing his partner. Giving up alcohol had left him with a feeling of emptiness nearly as great as Greg's death. In spite of his efforts to take pleasure in life again, all he came back to was one refrain: I'm just another pathetic, lonely, old queer. He gave a snort of contempt when he tried to substitute the new word they were using now: 'gay' for 'queer'. A lifetime of insults, behind-the-hand snickers and, once, a physical attack, made 'gay' a laughable attempt to cover an experience that for him had been anything but ludicrous. The only thing that had made it bearable was the twenty-five years with Greg which had ended with a gasp, his hand clutching his chest and collapse.

He turned his mind to the matter at hand, called the newspaper and dictated the ad: Room for Rent/Private Bath/Kitchen Privileges/Pool/ Single Person, then changed Person to 'Man'.

The ad ran the weekend, and he received several calls with three follow-up visits. The first man, in his thirties, looked thuggish and shifty-eyed, so he took his number and told him he was going to interview everyone first, then make his decision. He heard the man mutter 'faggot' under his breath on his way out.

The second person to visit was so obviously stoned that he knew the rent would always be somewhere in the future, so he gave him the same message.

The last person to show up was too young, 18 to 20, cocky, big scorpion tattoo on the right forearm. "I get to use the pool?"

"Yes, until midnight."

"Can I bring a girl over once in a while?"

He knew this was the inevitable consequence of renting a room, so he gritted his teeth. "Yes, but no late night partying. And two months' rent up front."

"You didn't say that in the ad."

"I forgot."

"Wow, man, is that a shower out there?" It was the shower Greg and he had built, surrounded by bananas and completely hidden from the street. His private life was being invaded.

"Yes, it's a shower."

"That's cool, a shower outside. Can I use it?"

"Yes."

"Okay, I'll take the room," and he pulled two month's rent, in cash, out of his pocket and handed it over. My name's Tommy, Tommy Smith," and he extended his hand.

"James," and he took the hand.

"When can I move in, Jim?"

"James, please. I don't like nicknames."

"Okay, James."

"You can move in anytime," he answered, though he wanted to say 'never.' Was he really going to share his beautiful home with a brash, unskillful teen-ager? Young as he was, though, perhaps his behavior would be easier to manage. "But there are rules," James said. "See this black floor? Take your shoes off outside. And you have to clean up after yourself in the kitchen. I cook a lot and you can't be in my way. Okay?"

"Okay, dude." James had never been called a 'dude' before and was unsure how to react to it. The youth headed towards the door to leave, then turned around. "This place is too cool. You're gay, ain't you?"

"Don't say ain't," was James' immediate response.

The boy laughed. "You're a teacher, ain't... *aren't* you? You're just like my teachers back in Georgia."

"Yes, I was a teacher for a while, and yes, I'm like *that*, but you don't have to worry. I will never approach you *that* way."

"Dude, I have gay friends, we all have. They don't try to touch the anaconda and everything's cool," and the boy laughed again and left.

When the boy was gone, James felt disturbed. He put on Monserrat Caballé's Butterfly and craved a bottle of compensation to help him through this. Why couldn't Greg have lived? He didn't want change and newness. He wanted a partner in the kitchen making the vinaigrette while he spun the greens dry. A man with whom he could argue Callas versus Sutherland.

Two days later, there was a knock on the gate. Three young men stood there and James' first reaction was fear. Then the kid walked up behind them. "Moving day." Then a yell: "Hey, shoes off, guys," as one of his friends started to walk inside.

James retreated inside and listened to them as they moved boxes in and Thomas—Tommy—showed them around the place and he heard their appreciation, vulgarly expressed: "Man, you're gonna get a lotta pussy here," was the most crude. And, once, he heard the inevitable question: "He's a fag. You gonna be Okay here?"

He heard the boy laugh. "He's cool, guys. He already told me I can have girlfriends over. Imagine a chick in this swimming pool at night," and he made the 'shark on its way' sound from the movie *Jaws* and they all laughed.

Then he smelled pot. Greg and he had indulged, but were always discreet, afraid of the legal consequences. He knew it was more liberal now, but he would have to have a talk with the boy when they were alone.

When they were all gone, he fixed himself dinner, left a note for Thomas—Tommy—on his bedroom door that there was food on a plate in the fridge if he wanted to re-heat it.

He awoke that night from a deep sleep because the downstairs door had opened. He heard footsteps back and forth and remembered he now had a tenant. He cracked his door to hear better, heard the fridge door open, then the microwave, then the clink of cutlery against china. Tommy had found his note. He closed his door and went back to sleep.

The next morning, he woke at his usual seven o'clock and went downstairs. All of the food he'd left was gone, and there was a piece of paper with a peasant's scrawl on top of the dirty dishes in the sink: "Awsome food, dude. Leve the dishes. I'll wash em."

The spelling was appalling, but he was touched that the boy had taken the trouble to write the note. He washed the dishes.

Tommy worked nights as a bar-back in one of the tourist bars downtown, so slept until noon every day, which left James his mornings to himself with the newspaper and the Cuban coffee he'd come to love, and time to plan the day and do some cooking before the boy—and he was still just a boy at 19—woke up and came downstairs.

They skirted carefully around each other for the first two weeks, James very careful to give the boy his space. Each time the boy's friends came over, James retreated upstairs, and he was particularly careful not to go outside when Tommy was using the outside shower.

One Sunday afternoon, James walked out on the back deck, unaware that Tommy had just finished his shower and was striding, completely naked, back to the house. James froze, terrified at being thought a voyeur. When Tommy caught sight of him, he laughed and started shimmying side to side to make his dick slap back and forth from one leg to another, banging his chest with his fists, as unself-conscious as a happy young animal. When James recovered from the shock, he couldn't help it, he started laughing, too. Tommy wrapped a towel around himself and gave James a friendly bump on his way back inside.

That night in bed, James played the scene over again in his mind, and was surprised to discover that the pleasure he had taken in it was more what?—fraternal?—paternal?—than carnal.

It broke the ice between them, and they began to spend a little time together, usually at meals James insisted Tommy sit down for. Slowly, he taught the boy manners and the need for them: close your mouth when you chew, use your cutlery this way—don't stab your food—then the education broadened out from there. James' atlas, always kept on the shelf under the coffee table was pulled out often as he told the boy about his and Greg's travels or in response to a question.

Tommy slowly revealed his history: a father in prison for life, an alcoholic mother, and these painful revelations awakened in James protective feelings he hadn't been aware of. James, in return, started telling Tommy bits and pieces of his own past, and about having been a teacher.

One night, the kid asked why James had quit teaching.

"I don't like talking about it, Tommy."

"Come on...I told you all that ugly shit about me."

James hesitated.

"Okay. I was an English teacher in a high school. It wasn't easy because some of the boys made fun of me for—well you know what." Tommy nodded. "But I love the language, and especially the literature, the writing, and I tried to show them the beauty of it. Sometimes, it seemed like I was getting through to a few.

"But there was one kid, big, a popular football player, Bill Benson—I'll never forget the

Wesley Sizemore

name. One day he'd been even more disruptive and disrespectful in class than usual, so I told him to stay after the other kids had left and told him I'd had enough and I was going to fail him if he didn't change."

"Fuck you," he told me and stormed out, and he used that word I hate."

"Faggot?"

"Yes." James looked away for a moment, remembering the insult.

"Two days later, I was called into the principal's office where Bill, his parents, and the principal all faced me. Bill claimed I had approached him sexually. To spare the school embarrassment, the principal said, I was being asked to leave and, if I agreed, they would give me my pension early. I took the offer and Greg and I moved here."

"No, man," Tommy yelled. "Why didn't you fight it? That ain't right."

"It was a different time."

Tommy shook his head in disbelief. "Not fair, dude," and he got up and put an arm around James and gave him a couple pats on the back. "You're good people."

James froze, unsure how to react to the touch, but Thomas, Tommy, didn't seem to notice.

***

Life settled into comfortable compromises, James happy to have another warm presence in the house, Tommy seemingly happy to have a place to show off to his friends and, especially, the abundance of girlfriends he brought home from the bar. James was always polite to the ones who stayed over.

Then late one Sunday morning, while James was lying on the sofa reading, Tommy stumbled downstairs alone and sat in the chair next to him. They were comfortable enough with each other now that there was no need to speak. James looked over and went back to reading.

Then it happened. Tommy, silent, walked over and curled himself up on James' body and lay there. James, paralyzed, didn't know what to do. This wasn't sexual, but a kind of needful touch unknown to him. He began to stroke the boy's head, and the boy burrowed deeper into his chest. They lay like that for how long? Minutes? Eternity? Then Tommy got up and went into the kitchen to fix himself something to eat as if the Earth hadn't shifted, moving every tectonic plate towards...what?

Frightened though he was by the experience, James realized how privileged he'd been to see into the soft heart of a child in need. He began playing even more parent/mentor to Tommy who soaked up the attention. James began to believe that life could again have meaning and pleasure. He had a son. How strange and wonderful was that.

Things began to change two months later. The usual banter between the two of them got edgier one day and James withdrew, hurt. Tommy withdrew, too, not seeking James out for days and when he did, there was an emotional distance that was new. The distance persisted until James asked Tommy one day if something was wrong.

"No, man. Nothing's wrong." But it was hollow, the answer.

James thought money was missing from his wallet once, and then one month, Tommy's rent was late, and he acted coldly indifferent when James confronted him. One day when Tommy was at work, James went into his room and found the proof of what he'd feared: the kid was doing cocaine.

When he confronted Tommy the next day, the boy became furious. "What were you doing in my room?"

"Tommy, if you're going to be doing cocaine and not paying your rent, you have to move out."

Tommy looked shocked by that. "Fuck it, then. I'll move out. I thought you were my friend."

"Tommy..."

"Fuck off and leave me alone. I'll move out tomorrow."

"Tommy..."

"Leave me alone, faggot."

Tommy moved out the next day and never came back, but the bottle did, slowly at first, then in the mind-numbing quantities necessary to block the loneliness.

A month later, James opened the paper to read that a shop owner downtown had called the police to report a man asleep against a dumpster behind his store. He was not asleep but dead. Thomas Smith, a corpse.

How could the kid who'd danced across a black floor, laughing, a life force, possibly be a corpse? He fell to the floor, sobbing, begging that it not be true.

But it was. Thomas Smith, 20 years old, identified by the scorpion tattoo on his right forearm. Heroin overdose.

Why hadn't he stood by the kid and make him get help instead of kicking him out?

Five days later, he had made his own decision. He put on Renata Tebaldi's version of 'O Mio Bambino Caro', pushed 'repeat', lay down on the sofa, and propped up two photos on the coffee table: the one of himself and Greg in front of the Eiffel Tower and another of himself and Tommy in front of Ft. Jefferson, a trip he had taken them on for Tommy's birthday. Walking Tommy through the fort and giving him the history of Dr. Mudd imprisoned there after setting Booth's leg following the assassination of president Lincoln.

The trip had given them both a joyful break from their routine life. He now placed the glass and forbidden bottle in reach and emptied the pills into his hand.

He hesitated. "If there is a god and this is a sin, I'm sorry." He touched Greg's photo first, then Tommy's, begging their forgiveness. He poured the glass full and stared at it a second, then drank it empty, using the liquid to swallow the first two pills.

It did not take long for the all-embracing warmth of the alcohol to bestow its familiar comfort. Another glass, two more pills, and the warmth increased, and he began to smile at the photos.

Another glass, hand a little unsteady now, and two more pills, and he sank back into the sofa, all fear gone now, giving himself up to the journey. And soon, they were both there, Greg and Tommy, friends already—how wonderful—standing over the sofa looking down at him and smiling. He smiled back and his hand reached up towards them, then fell back.

Afterword

When I began working on this project, my stories were not a part of it. Wesley approached me and said he wanted to work on a book. He'd been writing short stories for a while and thought that he had enough of them to put together a nice volume.

"Would you let me design it?" I asked while having a glass of wine on his porch on Fleming Street. I didn't go to school for graphic design. I honed my skills at secondary jobs after my two divorces from academia. I'm a teacher by trade, that's what I went to college for; but teachers are expendable for a multitude of reasons, twice I've lost my jobs and graphic design has been my fall back.

"Sure," Wesley said, not knowing what he was getting into. You don't know but getting into tight spaces and out of them is Wesley Sizemore's modus operandi. I got to work on the cover of the book while Wesley was deciding which stories to put in it. He decided on ten; the rest didn't make the cut.

"It's not enough for a book," he complained to me on the porch as we watched another sunset after my day job at the Key West Library. And yes, we were having wine.

"I thought you had twenty," I said. "I thought you said you had twenty-three. You boasted."

"When did I say that?" he queried, and picking up the bottle poured some more in my glass and added, "un poquito más?" demonstrating his ability for languages.

"Yes you did, and Ken was there!" I stated emphatically. Kenneth Michaels is a Key West writer and a dear friend. We have shared many evenings on the balcony at Fleming Street together.

"Well, fuck that. I don't remember it, what am I going to do now?"

"The fact that you don't remember it doesn't make it untrue. Have another sip of wine, Felicia. How about we write it together; you liked some of my stories and I'm more than happy to let you edit them." I jumped into the abyss headfirst.

"But I hate editing," he cried to the wind. "You have no idea how many projects are in my hands right now," he enumerated them; I'll protect the identities of the innocent.

"Ahh, you'll get over it, are you in or out?" I charged again.

"I'm in."

That was the beginning of a book of short stories. I have seen most of the stories before; I even have a couple in my computer. I wanted to make sure that they were the latest versions; he re-sent them to me. There were a couple of omissions, but the lot was solid. *Saying Good-bye to Reinaldo Arenas*, and *Birds of Paradise* were in, two of my favorites. I contributed six of mine; two of them about a character named David, a frustrated writer that I'm developing and I'm very fond of. *The House on Fleming Street*, which by now you have read, and *Nurse Irma*, which has a new character: Margarita Céspedes del Río, who came into my life a few days ago. I will write more about her for sure—she is real, maybe another short story, maybe a novel.

Another conversation on the porch on Fleming Street started. "How about an epigraph?" I asked.

"Are your stories completely fiction?"

"Yes, I think so. Even though they are rooted in my experiences, like yours are; I've fictionalized most of them. Yours are less fiction."

"I think you're right." Wesley concluded, "No, the epigraph I had in mind won't work." I shared with him the one I placed in my novel:

If the shortest distance between
two points is a line,
I will make it an arch, always.
Understanding this,
And embracing it;

It's my life journey.

"You're so queer," Wesley laughed, "un poquito más?"

"How about a 'Preface'? I can ask Ken to write it?"

"What in the world would you like to put in a 'Preface'?" Wesley asked giving me a sideways look.

Originally, I wanted Ken to write a comparison of our two writing styles without giving up too much of the stories to the readers. But then Ken turned the tables on me. A few months ago, when he published his second novel; he asked me to write a review for the local newspaper. I asked him to give me some pointers as to what he wanted me to say. So, when I asked him to write the preface; he answered with the same idea.

"Why don't you write down some notes for me?"

"Touché, clever little…" I said out loud when I read the email.

Then I thought that I wanted the reader to dive into the stories without any pre-conditions or preliminary thoughts. I moved the table of contents to the back of the book.

"Huh?" confusion written all over Wesley's face. "Why would you do something like that?"

"I changed my mind about it." I explicated, "I want the reader to go right into the short stories with a clear mind. And I want to write something about how to write a short story."

"What the fuck?" Wesley has a particular predilection for the word. "No, no, I want writing to remain a mystery."

"Are you fricking Proust?" I prefer to use a milder oath. Even though Wesley has a Master's degree in French Lit, we share a dislike for Proust and his pompous remembrance of the past. "And who in their right mind will place a table of contents at the back of a book?"

"Me!" I stated determined. "I did it in my first novel."

"Every single book I know has its table of content at the front." Wesley threw his hands into the air. "From all the fights that Mr. Alvarado could have picked up with the world of publishing, this is the one you're throwing your towel at?"

"Yes," I said, "and remember you agreed that I was designing the book." I smiled.

"Oh my God, what mess have I gotten into?" Wesley filled up his wine cup to the brim. He didn't pour for me, but I did.

The discussion about writing was on. I cited *Danse Macabre, On Writing*, by Stephen King; *Writing Down the Bones*, by Natalie Goldberg; and *Starting from Scratch,* by Rita Mae Brown. Wesley cited Flaubert's *Madame Bovary* and *Père Goriot* by Emile Zola; and surprised me with Miguel de

Unamuno's *How to Write a Novel.*

"Good job," I said. "Unamuno was the icing on the cake."

It was close to two o'clock in the morning. Stephen, my husband of twenty-seven years, was texting me on the phone. "Where are you?" I explained. "Really?" he texted back. "You're almost sixty-years old and you're behaving like you're in your twenties in Chicago." I tried to explain how today had fired me up, how I hadn't had a good literary argument in the last few years.

"Whatever," was the message that showed up in my phone's screen. He was pissed; I knew I was going to pay dearly for this one; but I was having too much fun.

The house on the left side of Wesley's is a bed and breakfast. The lady who was sleeping (maybe) closest to the porch had already come out her own porch and given us "the look." By now she was annoyed by our discussion, she came back out again:

"Would you two spare me the literature class? I'm on vacation."

Not missing a beat, Wesley asked, "Would you like a glass of wine?"

"Bourbon is my poison, do you mind my robe?" Impishly, "I'm an English Lit teacher."

"Come around, I'll set you up with a cheap one," Wesley answered. "The staircase door is open."

The bourbon was waiting for her.

"Hi guys, I'm Magdalene." She was well-versed and discussed with gusto. She refuted both of our arguments. We discussed characterization and dialogue; Julio Cortázar and Jorge Luis Borges. She cited Alice Munro's short stories, José Saramago's poetry and Baudelaire's *Fleurs du Mal*.

"But that's poetry," I protested, "How can you write short stories from poetry?"

"Have you read John Lahrs' latest bio about Tennessee Williams? Tenn wrote a poem, then a short story, then a play, what's wrong with you, hot shot?" She was marvelous.

"Checkmate!" I said.

"Well, I'm glad someone has put you in your place!" said Wesley, but he was interrupted.

"I'm not done yet, you are next," she flashed a beautiful smile, "It's five o'clock in the morning; where's breakfast around here?"

"I'm sorry but I need to go, someone is very angry at me right now. Enjoy the breakfast." As I was unlocking my bike, I heard Wesley proposing Pepe's for the next round of discussion. I called from the sidewalk, "Hey Wesley, how about an Afterword?"

"Whatever," he answered.

Key
West

Shorts

Key West Shorts